An Ocean Apart, a World Away

Also by Lensey Namioka

Ties That Bind, Ties That Break

An Ocean Apart, a World Away

A NOVEL BY

LENSEY NAMIOKA

DELACORTE PRESS

Published by
Delacorte Press
an imprint of
Random House Children's Books
a division of Random House, Inc.
1540 Broadway
New York, New York 10036

Visit us on the Web! www.randomhouse.com/teens
Educators and librarians, for a variety of teaching tools, visit us at
www.randomhouse.com/teachers

Cataloging-in-Publication Data is available from the Library of Congress.
ISBN 0-385-73002-0 (trade)—ISBN 0-385-90053-8 (lib. bdg.)

The text of this book is set in 14.5-point Perpetua.

Book design by Liney Li

Manufactured in the United States of America

June 2002

10 9 8 7 6 5 4 3 2 1

BVG

An Ocean Apart, a World Away

CHAPTER 1

"*I*t's out of the question!" said Father. I was usually able to coax him into seeing things my way, but this time he was firm. "Shanghai is one of the most disorderly cities in the world! Even in England, I heard people use the term 'to shanghai,' and it means . . ." He stopped, looked embarrassed, and then continued. "Anyway, it's an evil place. I can't allow a daughter of mine to be exposed to that wicked city without protection."

We continued eating, and nobody spoke for some minutes. Having lost my appetite, I just picked at the grains of rice in my bowl.

In a few days my dearest friend, Tao Ailin, was leaving on a steamship from Shanghai to America. It was possible that I would never see her again. I desperately wanted to say good-bye to her before the ship sailed.

Then Mother spoke, and to my surprise, she took my side. "Yanyan and Ailin were very close, and I can understand how much she wants to see her friend one last time."

Father thought for a while. "Very well, Yanyan can go to Shanghai if we find someone to accompany her as protector," he said finally. After a moment he said, "How about my secretary, Xiao Lin?"

"We cannot have Yanyan go to Shanghai accompanied by a man who is not a relation!" cried Mother, shocked.

"Besides, he's not much of a protector," I said. The secretary was a meek little man who would cringe in alarm if a cockroach crossed his path. "If a bully showed up, *I* would have to protect *him*!"

Help came from a most unexpected source. Eldest Brother cleared his throat. "Actually, I was thinking of going to Shanghai myself. My friend Liang Baoshu has some people he wants to meet there, and he asked if I would like to accompany him. Maybe Yanyan can come with us."

I had heard Eldest Brother mention Liang Baoshu before as a fellow student in his martial arts class. According to tradition, a well-educated gentleman should be good in both *wen,* meaning book learning, and *wu,* meaning martial skills. My two elder brothers had taken martial arts lessons from a master. Second Brother had dropped out after a while, but Eldest Brother continued the lessons, and we knew he was one of the best students in his class. The class had another outstanding student called Liang Baoshu, he had said.

My parents decided to invite Liang Baoshu for dinner the following night so that they could meet him and judge for themselves whether he would be a suitable companion for the trip to Shanghai. I was overjoyed. I had always been interested in the martial arts, and now I would meet one of the best students in the class. Best of all, I would have a chance to go to Shanghai and see Ailin after all.

●　　●　　●

"This is Liang Baoshu," said Eldest Brother, introducing his friend.

The boy bowed to my father first, then to my mother. He did not turn toward me, nor did Eldest Brother introduce me.

This allowed me to study the visitor. He was very tall, which made me suspect he was a northerner. Our family, the Zhangs, had lived in Nanjing for generations. Our city is about halfway up China, and *Nanjing* literally means "Southern Capital," while *Beijing* means

"Northern Capital." So we tended to think of ourselves as southerners. Most northerners were tall, with high cheekbones, and they had a reputation for being taciturn. They claimed they were people of deeds, not words. We southerners said they just couldn't express themselves very well.

Liang Baoshu was not only tall but moved with easy grace, and I could well believe that he was one of the best students in the martial arts class. When he spoke, I became certain that he was a northerner, because he had the accent of Beijing City.

We sat down to eat dinner, with the men on one side of the table and the women on the other side. I had heard that in some families, men and women were placed in alternate seats. We were modern, but not that modern!

As usual, I gave Mother my arm as she walked to the dining table. She had bound feet and tottered a little while she walked. After I had helped Mother sit down, I straightened up and found the visitor looking at my feet and then straight into my face.

"Didn't my brother tell you?" I said. "I don't have bound feet."

Liang Baoshu blinked at being addressed directly but recovered quickly. "Manchu women don't have bound feet, either," he said.

Father dominated the dinner conversation. Sometimes my brothers openly contradicted him, for unlike many Chinese fathers, he permitted his children to do this. He actually enjoyed arguing with us. Of course, he enjoyed winning the argument even more. Tonight he started talking about vehicles that were not pulled by men but powered by engines.

For once Mother joined the conversation. Usually she was too shy to speak out, especially when there were male guests present. But lately Father had been encouraging her to speak up. (The fact that I spoke out a lot had its effect on Mother, too.) "I thought we already had vehicles powered by engines," she said softly. "Don't they run on those iron roads that are being built all over the country? There's one that runs all the way from here to Beijing!"

"You're thinking of trains," said Father. "I mean something different. I'm talking about motorcars that carry only three to four people. They don't need iron tracks, but can run on regular roads. Mark my words, we'll see our streets full of these motorcars someday!"

The rest of us looked skeptical. I frankly couldn't imagine our streets jammed with these motorcars. The rickshaw men wouldn't stand for it, and think of the mess if one of these things should become tangled up with a mule cart!

Eldest Brother smiled at our guest. "The so-called motorcars might replace your beloved horses one day!"

Liang Baoshu smiled back. "Maybe they will in the city streets, but not in the wide-open countryside. There's nothing more exhilarating than riding a good horse."

His eyes were bright as he talked about riding, and I could easily picture him galloping like the wind. I must have been listening with my mouth open. Again he looked directly into my face.

I blushed and looked down. I didn't often blush, and I was almost never embarrassed, so I made an effort to raise my head and meet his eyes again. What was he seeing when he looked at me? I knew I was not beautiful. I didn't have what writers called cherry lips, moth-wing eyebrows, and plum-blossom cheeks. In fact, I thought my cheeks were too round. Mother liked to call me her cute little dumpling, but I couldn't trust the words of a mother. Besides, I didn't want to be a dumpling; I wanted to be a woman warrior, like the ones in the adventure novels I was always reading. I wondered if our guest liked girls who were bold and active.

When the meal was ended, Eldest Brother said he wanted to show his guest a book recommended by his teacher. Liang Baoshu bowed politely to my parents and thanked them for their hospitality. Before he left the table, he glanced at me once again. It was such a quick glance that I would have missed it if I hadn't been waiting for it.

The next day, my parents gave their approval to my trip to Shanghai with Eldest Brother and Liang Baoshu. I would be seeing Ailin again.

* * *

The night before we left for Shanghai, I thought back on my friendship with Tao Ailin. We had first met at the MacIntosh School, which was run by American missionaries. Ailin and I were among the few girls who did not have bound feet, and we had immediately become friends.

But Ailin's unbound feet caused her engagement to be broken. After her father died, the Tao family encountered financial problems, and Ailin's position at home became so intolerable that she left to work as a nanny for the Warners, an American missionary family.

My family, the Zhangs, was well-off because we had managed to keep our money even after the revolution in 1911. In the case of Ailin's family, their money had come largely from land that had been taken over by various warlords. It was now ten years after the revolution, but conditions in China were still very unstable. The central government controlled only a small part of the country, while the rest was dominated by powerful warlords, some of them no better than bandits.

It was one of the saddest days of my life when Ailin had to drop out of school after her uncle decided he could no longer pay the fees. During the two years Ailin worked for the Warners, I saw her only a few times. I think she avoided me and the rest of her former schoolmates. Our English teacher, Miss Gilbertson, once invited her to a party for her students. Ailin looked uncomfortable the whole time, and she never came to a gathering again. I tried inviting her to my house, but she would always say that her duties as a nanny kept her too busy to come. I gave up trying to press her.

And now Ailin was about to go to America with the Warners. She would cross the ocean and go to a country nearly at the other end of the world! A part of me envied her this great adventure. But going to America was not in my future. I already knew what I was going to do, and what my future was going to be.

Four years before, when I was twelve years old, I had decided I wanted to become a doctor. Our family doctor was a dignified gentleman with a long white beard. He would stroke his beard and talk in his deep voice about the philosophical aspects of various illnesses. I didn't understand anything he said, but I was deeply impressed by his manner.

To examine his patients, he felt the pulses in various parts of their body. In the case of a woman patient, he took the pulses in her arm, which she extended while she stayed hidden modestly behind the curtains of her bed. After feeling the pulses, he would diagnose the illness and prescribe an herbal medicine.

I used to be awed at the way the doctor could diagnose an illness simply by feeling some pulses. Then something happened that started me wondering. One of our maids got a deep cut in her hand, which became red and puffy. The family doctor was summoned, and as usual, he felt the pulses in her arm while offering his philosophical discourse. At the end, he prescribed a yellowish powder, which was mixed with hot water and given to the girl to drink.

My father looked on skeptically while the family doctor treated the maid. Father had traveled to Europe and lived for two years in London, working at the Chinese legation there. During that time he had become fascinated with Western science and medicine. In Europe, Father had heard that something with alcohol, such as a strong liquor, could help kill the poisons in a wound. After the family doctor had left, Father decided to try this new treatment. "Fetch me some strong liquor," he said to Mother.

Mother brought over a bottle of our best *wujiapi* liquor, and Father splashed some over the wound. The maid screamed and leaped out of bed, knocking over Mother and two other maids who were holding her down. She howled and shrieked for a while, and then fell into an exhausted sleep. After a few days, she began to recover.

I never forgot that incident. Was it the liquor that cured the maid? Or was it the powder from the old family doctor? How could there be such drastically different ways to treat a wound? That was when I resolved to become a doctor. I wanted to know about Western medicine, as well as traditional Chinese medicine.

From that day on, I tried to look on whenever the family physician visited someone at our residence. Pretty soon the doctor became annoyed by my nosiness, and once he actually ordered me out of the room. Although Father never again had *wujiapi* liquor splashed directly into a cut, he ordered it used to wipe the surrounding area whenever someone received a hurt. I eagerly took on the role of bringing the bottle of liquor, and even helped wipe the wound. After a while our people began to say that they really healed faster, and some even gave me credit for bringing them luck. I became convinced that alcohol, rather than the physician's yellow powder, was more effective for treating wounds.

By that time, I had already been attending the MacIntosh School for Girls, which was run by American missionaries. Some of our relatives found it shocking that I should be going to a school run by foreigners, where they would fill me with strange, modern ideas. "Things have been changing since the revolution," said

Father. "It's high time for Yanyan to be exposed to new and modern ideas."

I got into a lot of trouble in school because I was loud and liked to contradict the teachers. My teacher asked the class one day what we intended to do after leaving school. For once I won the teacher's approval, when I announced my ambition to study Western medicine.

My determination to study medicine had Father's support. He returned from Europe bringing fascinating Western instruments, including one called a microscope. He let me peer through its glass opening, and I saw some tiny things moving around. Father told me they were germs, and they were invisible to the naked eye. He said some of these germs could have caused our maid's hand to swell. He was pleased that I would be able to learn about germs one day.

There were a number of modern, Western-style hospitals in China, most of them set up with foreign help. Some even had women doctors, trained in Japan, Europe, and America. They dealt mostly with problems of childbirth, but I heard Father mention one woman doctor who became a surgeon and actually cut people open with a sharp knife called a scalpel! She sounded like a true heroine, and I wondered if I could ever become a doctor like her.

"Working as a doctor would ruin Yanyan's chances

of getting married!" declared my aunt, one of our more conservative relatives. "No decent gentleman would want to marry a woman who worked outside the home."

"I don't intend to get married," I declared. "I'm going to earn a living by my work."

And I felt that way still—at least until I met Liang Baoshu.

* * *

The journey from Nanjing to Shanghai was about forty-five miles, and it would take five hours. This was only my second train trip. The first was a group outing of our class last year, when we had been taken to visit the famous gardens of Suzhou. We had been crowded into compartments with eight girls in each, and I still remembered the high-pitched noise of the other girls' chattering. One girl in our group became sick, and we had to open a window to let her throw up. Unfortunately, some of the vomit blew back inside, and this made several other girls sick, too. It was not a trip I wanted to remember.

But this trip was different. Although the purpose was a sad one—seeing off my friend—the journey itself was much more comfortable. We were in a first-class compartment, and for a while the three of us had the little room to ourselves. I had a window seat, and

Eldest Brother sat next to me. Liang Baoshu was seated opposite me, and at first I was too shy to look up into his eyes.

The compartment became uncomfortably warm and I tried to open the window, but I couldn't raise it. Liang Baoshu stood up, jerked at the window, and got it halfway open. At that moment, the train gave a loud toot and a lurch. We both staggered. Just as we regained our balance, a black cloud of soot from the coal-burning engine blew straight into our faces.

After I finished coughing, I opened my eyes and saw a stranger with a black face laughing hysterically. I looked again and saw that it was Liang Baoshu. He took a breath, pointed at my face, and broke into another fit of laughter. I realized that my face was just as black as his.

Dipping a handkerchief into my cup of tea, I tried to wipe the soot from my face, but only succeded in smearing it. Liang Baoshu did the same, and judging from smudges still left on his face, I gathered that I looked just as bad. Eldest Brother grinned broadly as he surveyed the two of us, and told us that we both resembled street ragamuffins.

After that, I lost my shyness and relaxed. Before too long I found I was hungry. We stopped at a station, and I saw people selling food on the platform. When one of the vendors saw my nose pressed against the glass, he grinned and held up a bowl of soup noodles. I looked at Eldest Brother, but he shook his head. "Better not take a chance. You never know how clean the food is from these vendors."

"There's a dining room aboard the train," said Liang Baoshu, smiling at me. "We can eat lunch in a proper manner."

The thought of eating in a room full of strangers was exciting, although Mother would have turned pale at the very idea. I wanted to know how I could clean my face before appearing in public. Again, Liang Baoshu knew the answer. I had the impression that he was an experienced traveler. "There is a washroom at the end of this car. You'll find basins and a supply of water. There's even a mirror."

I found not only a washroom, but also a toilet. Having used a flush toilet at the MacIntosh School, I was able to manage without disgracing myself.

The three of us, looking reasonably clean, went into the dining car, which had small rectangular tables covered with white linen cloths. A man in a white jacket ushered us to a table, and his eyebrows rose when he saw that I had unbound feet. He probably thought I was some sort of maid, accompanying the two boys to serve them.

Eldest Brother noticed the man's expression, and his

lips tightened with anger. I suspected that he was already sorry he had suggested taking me.

But our mood improved when we sat down and ordered food. Liang Baoshu did the ordering of the dishes. At first I was totally occupied by the novelty of dining in public and eating food presented by a stranger. After a while I began to ask Liang Baoshu about Shanghai, which he had apparently visited a number of times.

"The most noticeable thing about Shanghai is its foreign influence," he said. He added bitterly, "In fact, certain zoned areas in the city are under the control of Western powers."

"Is it true that a foreigner who commits a crime won't be punished if it happens in the foreign sector?" I asked. "It's like having our country occupied by alien conquerors!"

"That's exactly what it's like," said Eldest Brother, stabbing his chopsticks fiercely into a piece of pork. "Various parts of our country *are* being occupied."

"Well, it's not the first time," I said, sighing. "After all, the Mongols conquered us in the thirteenth century and set up the Yuan dynasty. Then we got conquered by the Manchus, who set up the Qing dynasty. We didn't get rid of them until the revolution ten years ago."

Eldest Brother stiffened. I wondered if I had said something wrong. Then I glanced at Liang Baoshu and saw that his face was also stiff and expressionless. Silently, he helped himself to some stir-fried bean sprouts.

Finally Eldest Brother broke the silence. "Well, at least being governed by the Manchus was better than being governed by a bunch of Westerners with big noses and straw-colored hair!"

We finished our meal, which was on the simple side. But at least it filled us, and we returned to our compartment. Inside, we found that there was another occupant: a man with a big nose and straw-colored hair.

He was stowing his luggage in the overhead rack, and when we entered, he smiled at us. "All right if I share the compartment?" he asked in English.

I had studied English for several years at the MacIntosh School, and while I didn't have the fluency of my friend Ailin, I could understand a fair amount. Eldest Brother and Liang Baoshu didn't know any English, but the newcomer's question was obvious.

So we nodded. It was inconvenient to lose our privacy, but we had no claim to the extra space.

As the newcomer finished stowing his luggage and sat down, Eldest Brother said softly, "What happens when these Big Noses catch a cold? They'd have to put a basin under their chin to catch all the catarrh."

I glanced nervously at the Westerner. He didn't say anything, and merely smiled briefly at each of us in turn. Then he took out an English newspaper, crossed his legs, and began to read.

Eldest Brother and Liang Baoshu started to discuss all the peculiarities of foreigners. Since they had contact with very few, the two of them simply repeated rumors they had heard.

"Foreigners are physically incapable of speaking Chinese," said Eldest Brother. "Something about the shape of their noses, perhaps."

"They can't appreciate subtlety in art," said Liang Baoshu. "Their eyes are set too deep, so they're unable to see the fine shading in a brush painting. That's why Western oil paintings are full of flat patches of bright color."

Eldest Brother and Liang Baoshu continued in that vein, commenting that foreigners needed to eat bloody meat at every meal, that they were so hairy they had to shave twice a day, that the women wore a small steel fence around their waist to keep it from expanding. . . .

I began to feel uncomfortable. Although I had met very few foreign men, I did see foreign women every day in school, and none of them wore a steel fence. Again I glanced at the man sitting next to me. He seemed totally immersed in his newspaper.

Finally I decided to change the subject. "Will I get to the docks in time to see Ailin off? When does the *Empress of Canada* sail, do you know?"

"We'll take a rickshaw as soon as the train arrives," said Liang Baoshu. "Don't worry, we're almost there. We'll get you to the ship in time."

"I'd give anything to go with Ailin to America," I said wistfully. "It's such a young country, and my teacher says that none of the cities in the western part is more than a hundred years old!"

"The country is so new that in some parts there are still savages with red skin," said Eldest Brother. "You'd better be careful, because they grab you by the hair and cut off your scalp!"

He was grinning as he said this, so I couldn't tell if he was serious or not about those red-skinned savages. Actually, I probably knew as much about America as Eldest Brother—maybe more. But before I could say anything, the train began to slow. We were about to arrive.

By the time the train was nearing the station, we had gathered our belongings and were ready to get off. The Westerner had his luggage in hand, and just before he went out to the corridor, he turned to us. "By the way," he said in excellent Chinese, "you don't have to worry about those red-skinned natives cutting off your scalp.

And their skin isn't really red. It's—well—not that different in color from yours."

We stared at him, and the three of *us* were the ones with red skin. I felt wave after wave of heat pass over my face. I didn't know where to look at first, and finally raised my eyes to look at the two boys.

Eldest Brother was biting his lower lip in mortification, and even Liang Baoshu had lost his usual self-possession. Somehow he looked more human that way, and I liked him better. He was the first to recover. "I'm sorry," he said to the Westerner. "I didn't know you could understand us—although that's no excuse for our rudeness, of course."

"That's all right," said the Westerner. His blue eyes were bright with laughter as he surveyed the three of us.

We still had a few minutes before we could get off, and to fill in the awkward interval, I asked the man where in China he was staying. "My wife and I have been living in Nanjing this past year, but we're going back to the States in a couple of months. You're all from Nanjing, aren't you?"

When we said yes, his expression became thoughtful. Putting his hand into the breast pocket of his suit, he took out a calling card and handed it to Liang Baoshu. "This is my address in Nanjing. Back in

America, I live in a small town in upstate New York. It's called Ithaca, and if you're ever there, look me up."

We finally arrived, and after stepping down onto the platform of the station, we saw the figure of the Westerner disappear. "I don't think I'll have any use for this," muttered Liang Baoshu after reading the name card. He was probably still smarting from having made a fool of himself with the American.

I took the card from him. "Wait, I want to find out what his name is. I'm curious about him." I peered at the small white card and saw that one side was in English and the other side in Chinese. "His name is George Pettigrew," I said, reading the card. "And he is a professor of Oriental history at Cornell University, whatever that is. Apparently it's in the city of Ithaca, in New York."

I slipped the card into my pocket, although, like Liang Baoshu, I didn't see that I would ever have any use for it.

CHAPTER 2

We did get to the docks before the *Empress of Canada* sailed, but without much time to spare. The ship looked immense, almost like a small city. I had taken trips up the Yangtze River with my parents, but we had been in wooden boats accommodating fewer than forty people. This iron ship in front of me seemed to hold hundreds of people. How could I ever hope to find Ailin among the passengers?

I anxiously scanned the faces of the people who were standing at the railing waving to friends below. Suddenly I saw her! Ailin was standing there alone, looking so forlorn that my heart went out to her. I shouted, and she started to wave. She had seen me too!

"I'm going aboard to talk to Ailin," I said to Eldest Brother. "Can you wait for me here?"

He nodded, and I began to thrust my way up the gangplank. By the time I reached the top, Ailin was right there, waiting for me. Tears streamed down our faces, and we couldn't speak at first because our throats felt too thick.

"You've cut your hair," Ailin finally said.

"Is that all you can say?" I demanded. "After all the trouble I took to see you?"

"How did you know I was going abroad?" asked Ailin.

"I heard the news from Miss Gilbertson," I said. Ailin had been the star pupil in our English class, and the teacher, Miss Gilbertson, had kept in touch with her after Ailin dropped out of school two years ago.

"The Warners wanted me to go with them and help with the children," said Ailin. "After years of living in China, they may have some trouble adjusting to American schools."

Ailin was slim and willowy, and she looked like the sort of frail beauty I read about in novels. It took courage for her to break ties with her family and go to work for a foreign missionary family. This trip to America was not a vacation, but was part of her work as a nanny. It was a wonderful treat, but she had worked hard to earn it.

There was a loud toot. It was time for the ship to leave. Suddenly I felt very wistful. "I'd better get off the ship, or I might wind up going with you to America."

Ailin smiled. "Well, why not?"

I wanted to trade places with Ailin, despite all her hardships. "How I envy you! You're embarking on a great adventure!"

Another loud toot, and I turned toward the gangplank. Then I remembered something. "I almost forgot! In fact, this was one of the reasons for coming." I took out a bag of money her uncle had given me to hand over to Ailin.

She stared. "You saw Big Uncle? You actually went to his den? That took courage!"

I laughed. "And I survived the experience—barely."

Ailin looked silently at the bag of money. Her uncle was the one who had refused to pay her school fees, and he was the reason she had left home. "Why did he give me the money?" she murmured, almost to herself.

"I guess he wanted to make sure that a daughter of the Tao family would have suitable accommodations," I said. I took one last look at my friend, and again I felt tears welling up. "Please don't forget to write to me, Ailin," I begged, and squeezed her hand hard.

● ● ●

The two boys and I watched the ship pull away from the docks. I couldn't bear to tear myself away as long as I could still see Ailin standing at the railing. But when the ship changed direction and I could no longer see her, I turned to leave. Eldest Brother looked impatient, and I remembered that Liang Baoshu had to meet some people and attend to other business in Shanghai.

We looked for a rickshaw to take us to our hotel but discovered that they had all been taken already by people seeing off their friends. We decided to walk toward the center of the city, where our chances of finding a free rickshaw would be better.

I was looking forward to the prospect of staying at a Western-style hotel. In Nanjing I had gone to one such modern hotel with my parents to visit a friend of Father's from England. That was several years ago, and my English had been too poor at the time for me to understand much. This time I would be spending the night at a hotel, and in my very own room! I almost shivered with excitement.

Thinking about the hotel, I didn't pay much attention at first to the street where we were walking. Then I heard Eldest Brother muttering, "Maybe it was a mistake to go this way."

I peered around at the street and saw that it was filthy. On both sides were beggars huddled against the walls. We had beggars in Nanjing, too, but I didn't often visit the parts of town where they were to be found. I saw that some of these beggars were disfigured and covered with sores. Would it help heal the sores to rub the skin with something containing alcohol? I wondered. I stopped in front of one beggar to throw him some coins and to have a closer look at a huge open sore on his nose.

Eldest Brother pulled me after him. "There's no time for that! We have to hurry."

We turned abruptly into an alley. "Too late!" said Liang Baoshu.

I followed his glance and saw that at the end of the alley, blocking our way, stood several figures. Behind me, Eldest Brother grunted, and I turned to see that more figures had appeared behind us. We were completely cut off.

"Well, well, what have we here?" said one of the men in front of us. He opened his mouth in a wide grin, and I saw that almost all of his front teeth were broken. "Which one of you young gentlemen owns this juicy little morsel?"

Some of the other men laughed, and I guessed that the man with the broken teeth was their leader. On his fractured mouth his grin widened. "Do you mind if we borrow her for a while this evening?"

Then I realized that *I* was the juicy little morsel he

was referring to. It made me so furious that I forgot to be frightened. I glanced at Eldest Brother and saw that his face was rigid with anger. He took a deep breath and began to roll up his sleeves. I realized then that he expected to fight. That was when I began to be afraid.

I turned to look at Liang Baoshu and saw that he had already rolled up his sleeves. His eyes were narrowed, but otherwise he looked the way he usually did.

"Oh, my," said the man with the broken teeth. "I see that these two young gentlemen want a scuffle. We don't want to disappoint them, now, do we?"

"Flatten yourself against the wall," Liang Baoshu whispered to me. "You can help us best by not moving a finger."

I swallowed and nodded, although I wanted to roll up my sleeves too, just to show these hoodlums that I was not afraid of them.

The leader turned to a hulking man standing next to him, who still kept the prerevolutionary hairstyle of a shaved forehead and long pigtail. "You're impatient, aren't you? Why don't you go first?"

The pigtailed man nodded and walked forward. For such a big man he moved very lightly, and I could tell that he had had some martial arts training. I opened my mouth and then realized that of course Liang Baoshu didn't need my warning.

The attack came much faster than I expected, but not too fast for me to follow the sequence of moves. The pigtailed man struck out at Liang Baoshu with his right fist. It was a feint, and at the last moment he swiveled and swung out with his left fist.

Liang Baoshu seemed to melt. He sank below the other man's fist and pivoted on one leg. Then he kicked his other leg right into his attacker's chest, which was left open when the man swung his arm. The pigtailed man gave a huge whoosh and collapsed against the wall.

For a moment there was silence in the narrow alley except for the pigtailed man's gasps. Then I heard a rustle behind me and saw that one of the men at my end of the alley was rushing at Eldest Brother.

Again I had to stifle the urge to shout a warning. My role was to stay out of the way and not do anything distracting.

My warning would have been unnecessary, in any case. Eldest Brother was fully alert to the danger. He began to move with dreamlike slowness, and I wanted to yell to him to hurry up. But he had all the time he needed to meet the attack. He dodged under a kick aimed at his neck, and while his attacker was still off balance, he seized the man by the collar and slammed him against the wall.

The attacker's two companions turned and ran. Eldest Brother and I exchanged a quick, grim smile. The danger at this end of the alley was over.

I looked over at the other end and saw that Liang Baoshu was having little difficulty dealing with his second opponent. Then I glanced at the leader of the pack, the man with the broken teeth. He was smaller in build than his followers. Did that mean he was a much more highly trained fighter? Then I saw his hand reach under his jacket and take something out.

"He's got a gun!" I yelled.

I was not the first to see the gun—not even the second. Before the words were out of my mouth, Eldest Brother had already rushed forward in a low crouch toward the other end of the alley. But he was too late to affect the outcome.

Liang Baoshu had picked up his opponent and thrown him straight at the leader just as the gun went off. This was the first time I had heard a gun at such close quarters, and the loud bang was deafening and left me stunned.

When I was finally able to look around, I saw that the shot had gone wild. The leader of the pack picked himself up from the ground, opened and closed his mouth a few times, then suddenly turned and ran. His followers stumbled after him.

The two boys rolled down their sleeves and straightened their clothes. Eldest Brother gave me a faint smile. That was his way of expressing approval for my not giving in to panic and getting in their way. It was true that even when things looked ugly, I hadn't been frightened—well, not truly frightened.

I turned to Liang Baoshu. "When the man with the pigtail attacked you, you used the Shandong style to counter him, didn't you?"

His mouth dropped open in surprise. I felt a spurt of pleasure at startling someone as self-possessed as he was. Then he recovered. "You know about the various styles of boxing?"

I would have liked to pretend to be a real expert, but with Eldest Brother looking on, it wouldn't have worked. "I like to eavesdrop on my brothers when they talk about their martial arts lessons," I confessed. "In fact, I'd love to take lessons myself."

Liang Baoshu's eyes widened, and I saw admiration in them. "You weren't frightened, were you? You even had time to notice my fighting style! With your spirit, you can certainly take lessons in the martial arts. I know some women who have become quite formidable."

He admired my spirit! It made me happier than if he had admired my looks. I had to turn my head away to hide my wide grin.

We reached the end of the alley and found ourselves

in a street. Coming toward us were four policemen, all Westerners.

"I heard a shot!" the officer barked at us. "What were you doing in that alley?"

From his accent, I realized that we were in the district of Shanghai controlled by the British. The English I learned at the MacIntosh School was American, but it was close enough to the British variety for me to understand the officer.

Eldest Brother and Liang Baoshu looked blank, since neither of them had studied English. It seemed that I would have to do all the talking. I cleared my throat. "We were walking toward our hotel, since we couldn't find a rickshaw. Then some, uh, bad men attacked us. One of them had a gun. Fortunately he didn't hit anybody. That shot must have been what you heard."

The officer looked skeptical. He didn't see how we had escaped unharmed when we had been attacked by a gang, one of them holding a gun. Although it was wholly against my nature, I decided it was time to put on the helpless female act. "I'm so glad you came to our rescue, Officer. I was so frightened!"

One of the policemen spoke to the officer. "We did see some pretty unsavory types slinking away just now, sir. Maybe they saw us coming."

The officer finally nodded. "That must have been it."

He turned and looked us over. "These two chaps don't seem very talkative, do they?"

"My brothers don't speak English," I told him. I decided to include Liang Baoshu as a brother, just to make things simpler for the policemen.

"But you do, eh?" asked the officer.

"I attend the MacIntosh missionary school in Nanjing," I said, and added with a simper, "What do you think of my accent?"

Perhaps the simper was overdoing things a bit, but it worked on the officer, and a couple of the men chuckled. "Your accent is pretty good, miss, even if it *is* American," said one.

"Right!" said the officer. "We needn't bother you any further, then."

The policemen started to walk away, but the officer turned back. "If you take my advice, you'd better get out of this unsavory neighborhood as soon as possible."

We continued our way along the street, which was better lit and cleaner looking than the alley. The two boys said nothing, and I could tell that they were both in a foul mood. Actually, I felt I had acquitted myself rather well in disarming the suspicions of the police. And the boys should have been proud of the way they had driven off the hoodlums. So why were they angry?

"The arrogance of those policemen!" Eldest Brother

said, finally breaking his silence. "They think they own this country!"

"Not the whole country, just the British sector here," I reminded him. "The French and the Americans control other sectors of Shanghai."

After our defeat in the Second Opium War, various foreign countries discovered how weak China really was. Among other humiliations, Britain and the United States forced China to give them control over various parts of Shanghai. France followed their example and carved out a French quarter in the city. All three did the same in several other cities convenient for their commercial and military purposes.

It was a continual source of national shame and resentment that we had been made to hand over parts of our country to outsiders. When we came in contact with foreign police maintaining order in these areas, we always had the feeling of being a conquered people. At least I had mustered enough English to talk to those British policemen as equals. I didn't know what I would have done if we had been in the French sector.

When Liang Baoshu broke his silence, I found out that he was in a bad humor for a different reason. "I really have to learn English," he growled.

I looked at him curiously. "Do you know any other language?"

"I know some Japanese and Korean, because they are

distantly related to Manchu," he replied. He added sourly, "I never thought English would be useful. It seems I was wrong!"

We were nearly at our hotel before I understood why he was so annoyed at not knowing English. He hated having to stand by helplessly while I did all the talking with the policemen.

* * *

We were staying at the Great Southern Hotel. Mother had been uneasy about my staying overnight at a hotel—in fact, she had been uneasy about the propriety of whole trip. But Father had given his permission. "Let Yanyan go. She should be safe enough with the two boys looking after her." (I resolved never to tell him about our encounter with the hoodlums in the alley.)

"But Yanyan can't sleep in the same room with the boys!" said Mother. We had gone on trips to the mountains and stayed at temple guest rooms. At those times, our whole family shared a room. But this time there was Liang Baoshu, who was not a family member.

Father thought for a moment. "Let the two boys share a room, and Yanyan can have her own room."

So there I was, in a room with Western-style furniture. There was a fat, fabric-covered chair and a bed so big and immovable that it seemed rooted to the floor. But what made me hug myself with glee was that this exotic room was all my own! How could I possibly sleep, with so many fascinating things to examine?

There was a knock on my door just as I was studying an enamel vessel, trying to decide whether it was a bedpan or a spittoon. I went to the door and opened it to find Eldest Brother standing outside. He frowned at me. "Don't open the door to anybody who knocks. Find out who it is first."

"Yes, Eldest Brother," I said meekly.

"Come on, let's go down to the dining room," said Eldest Brother. "It's late, and I'm hungry."

As soon as he said this, I realized that I was famished. Lunch on the train seemed ages ago. "Where is Liang Baoshu?" I asked.

Eldest Brother didn't answer at first. We sat down at a table, and he began to study the menu. "He's not eating with us," he replied, not looking up.

Then I remembered that the reason Liang Baoshu had come with us was because there were people in Shanghai he wanted to meet. "You're not going with him to meet his friends, then?" I asked.

"No!" said Eldest Brother. "What he does has nothing to do with me. And it's none of your business, either!"

It was unlike Eldest Brother to snap at me like this. Second Brother found me a nuisance, but Eldest Brother was usually more patient with me. After our adventure in the alley, I really thought I had earned his approval.

Then I realized that Eldest Brother was fidgeting because he was uncomfortable. He had come to Shanghai at the invitation of Liang Baoshu, but he had decided not to accompany his friend to the meeting after all. Was it because he didn't want to leave me alone at the hotel? No, I decided that was not the reason. The subject was a sensitive one he did not want to discuss. My guess was that his uneasiness had to do with Liang Baoshu and the mysterious meeting he was attending.

Eldest Brother gave his orders to the waiter. After the food arrived, I was so immersed in eating that I had no time to think of anything else. We had braised prawns, a steamed fish, and stir-fried chicken breast. I felt very adult, and I assumed the role of a hostess by putting food in Eldest Brother's rice bowl.

"Never mind," he said as I heaped more prawns over his rice. "I can help myself to the food."

All the better, I thought, and went back to my own food. After we had been eating silently for some minutes, a thought suddenly occurred to me. "Liang Baoshu said that he can speak some Japanese and Korean because they are distantly related to Manchu. Does that mean he speaks Manchu?"

Eldest Brother dropped his spoon into the soup bowl, and some of the liquid splashed onto his shirt. He muttered angrily under his breath and dabbed at it. Then he looked up at me. "He speaks it because his mother is Manchu."

I was so startled that I dropped my chopsticks. They rolled off my lap and onto the floor. A waiter came over and mopped up Eldest Brother's spilled soup, and handed me another pair of chopsticks. He must have thought that we were unusually clumsy.

So Liang Baoshu was half Manchu. Now that I knew, I realized that the clues were there. Recalling the conversation at dinner when he came to our house, I knew that he loved riding horses. He was tall, with the high cheekbones characteristic of northern Chinese but even more common among the Manchus.

The Manchus had conquered China in the mid-seventeenth century and founded the Qing dynasty, which ruled our country until the revolution of 1911. That was ten years ago, when I was six years old, but I still remembered the suspense, the anxiety, and the excitement that we all felt at the overthrow of the Manchu dynasty and the founding of our republic.

Eldest Brother bitterly resented the British policemen we had encountered because they were aliens who controlled a sector of Shanghai. The Manchus were aliens who had conquered our country and controlled it for more than two and a half centuries. How did Eldest Brother feel about someone who was half Manchu, then?

As I finished the last of my rice, I examined my own feelings toward Liang Baoshu. Somehow I couldn't think of him as one of the enemy aliens who had once conquered our country. He was only half Manchu, after all. In manner and in culture, he seemed totally Chinese.

Who were the people he was meeting this evening? Were they Manchus? There were two things I couldn't help remembering: One was that during Liang Baoshu's first visit to our house, he had seen that my feet were unbound, and he had told me that Manchu women did not have bound feet either. The other was the look of admiration in his eyes when I showed my interest in the martial arts.

*　*　*

When we returned from our trip to Shanghai, I finally convinced Eldest Brother to teach me some kung fu. "You never know what can happen these days," I said. "Our country is still unsettled, and we may not be safe even in the streets of Nanjing. I might meet some unruly types on my way home from school, for instance."

"If Yanyan meets any unruly types, the only decent thing for her to do is to run away immediately!"

snapped Second Brother. "If you teach her any kung fu, Eldest Brother, *she* will become an unruly type. In fact, she is one already!"

But Eldest Brother agreed with me that I should learn at least some basic techniques of self-defense. We started practicing in one of our courtyards, to the great amusement of the servants. They always cheered me on whenever they thought I made a good move. After a few weeks, Eldest Brother admitted that I was a good pupil. I wondered what Liang Baoshu would think if he saw me now.

CHAPTER 3

I told my English teacher, Miss Gilbertson, about my trip to Shanghai to see Tao Ailin. She wanted to know all the details because she had been very fond of Ailin, whom she considered one of her star pupils.

I also told Miss Gilbertson about my encounter with the British policemen. "I was so glad I attended your class! The officer thought of us as scum at first, but when I started speaking to him in English, he began to treat us like decent people!"

Miss Gilbertson made no comment about the behavior of the policemen. The teachers at our school avoided the whole sensitive subject of foreigners' controlling parts of Shanghai and several other Chinese cities. Even Miss Scott, our history teacher, glossed over the Opium War, the Boxer Rebellion, and other humiliating defeats suffered by the Chinese. This was frustrating for me. I wanted her to bring up these subjects so that I could have a good, fiery debate with her.

Maybe this was just as well. I was in my last year at the MacIntosh School, and it was time to work hard and avoid trouble. If I wanted to attend college and prepare for going to medical school later, I had to behave myself and get good grades and recommendations from my teachers.

My best subjects were mathematics and the sciences, but after the experience with the policemen in Shanghai, I began to focus more on my English studies. I thought of the American man we had met on the train. Maybe his tones were not quite accurate, but otherwise his Chinese was very good, in spite of the shape of his nose. If an American could master Chinese, I could certainly master English. Miss Gilbertson noticed my improvement and encouraged me. I didn't have Tao Ailin's wonderful ear, but I tried to make up for it with hard work.

* * *

In the months that followed, Liang Baoshu came to eat dinner with us a number of times. Mother didn't raise a fuss when I openly chatted with him at the dinner table. She only murmured a mild objection when I went to my brothers' rooms after dinner. "It's indecent for Yanyan to join a conversation with the boys!" she hissed as I started to follow my brothers to their rooms.

Father looked at things differently and made his usual comment about the changing times. "What was unthinkable before is now accepted even in many of the best families. Besides, nothing scandalous can happen when the girl's brothers and servants are all present."

Nevertheless, I suspected that Mother questioned the servants closely about my behavior during these talks. She seemed to be satisfied with their reports.

What the boys discussed most often was the career each of them intended to pursue. Eldest Brother and Liang Baoshu were both nineteen years old, and Second Brother was eighteen. They would soon finish their classical studies with their teacher.

"Things were simple in the old days," sighed Eldest Brother. "Any young man of good family studied for the government examinations."

This system of examinations had been established nearly a thousand years ago for selecting able young men as government officials, or mandarins. Since my brothers were both studious and intelligent, their chances of passing the examinations would have been excellent. The fact that our family was wealthy and influential would also have helped them to good appointments, although in principle only real ability mattered.

"Well, we have to face the fact that things are now different," said Liang Baoshu. His words seemed to echo Father's. "But even if the examination system is abolished, we still need able men for government positions."

My brothers and Liang Baoshu discussed the various ways of getting an official job. "With things all muddled these days," complained Eldest Brother, "the only sure way of getting a position is to offer a hefty bribe."

"I'm not sure I want to be an official, anyway," said Second Brother. "Maybe I'll try to get a job as a teacher at one of these academies for advanced learning that are being set up."

"By academies, you mean universities?" I asked, using the English word.

Second Brother hadn't heard of universities, but Liang Baoshu knew the word. "I understand these so-called universities are patterned after British and American institutions," he said. I knew that he had begun to study English. He had even tried out a few phrases with me. He turned to Second Brother. "If you hope to get a job at one of these, you'll have to study some of those modern subjects you dislike so much."

"I don't enjoy science or mathematics," said Second Brother, turning to me and making a face, "subjects that you like so much. But surely even modern universities still have to teach Chinese writing, history, and philosophy. After all, we had a political revolution, not a cultural revolution. We don't have to give up on our country's history, literature, and culture!"

"I think I'd like a job in a state library," said Eldest Brother. "Fortunately, the revolutionaries didn't burn all the old books, as Emperor Quin Shihuang did when he came to power." He turned to Liang Baoshu. "What are you planning to do?"

Our guest was silent for a moment and thoughtfully studied the teacup in his hand. Finally he raised his eyes. "I think I'd like to go into diplomatic service . . . work in a foreign consulate or legation . . . something like that."

"That's exactly what my father did!" I exclaimed. Father would be pleased at hearing this, and his opinion of Liang Baoshu would rise even further. "He was in England for several years, and he also worked in France."

Liang Baoshu smiled. "Well, I wasn't thinking of a European country. I'll probably try to find a position in India, Japan . . . one of the Asian countries." He turned to me. "And what do you plan to do when you finish school?"

"This stupid girl says she wants to be a doctor!" said Second Brother. He still regarded me as a noisy brat with silly ideas.

"She could probably do it, too," said Eldest Brother.

"She works very hard in school, and she might be able to enter one of those modern, uh, universities after she graduates from the missionary school."

Since our trip to Shanghai, Eldest Brother had begun to look at me with greater approval. Maybe it was because he remembered my coolness during the fight in the alley. Maybe it was because his friend Liang Baoshu seemed to approve of me. I think he noticed that Liang Baoshu and I were attracted to each other. Perhaps *attracted* was too strong a word. We were interested, let's say. Eldest Brother was pleased by this development.

He wasn't the only person to notice that Liang Baoshu and I were interested in each other. I was sitting on a china stool in our courtyard one day, doing my homework. It was late spring, and our jasmine bush was in full bloom. I couldn't resist sitting outside, where I could smell the fragrant white flowers. It was so pleasant that I closed my notebook and just luxuriated in the warmth and the fragrance.

Then I heard the voices of Father and Mother. They were on the other side of the bush and couldn't see me. "It's scandalous, letting them meet like this without a matchmaker acting as an intermediary!" said Mother.

"Times have changed, and we must change, too," said

Father, as he always did when Mother complained about current happenings.

"But we don't know anything about the boy," said Mother. "Well, we know that his mother is Manchu. I hardly call that a recommendation!"

Then I knew that they were talking about me and Liang Baoshu. A matchmaker! I hadn't realized that things had gone that far—or that my parents *thought* things had gone that far. I felt my face growing hot, and I tried to shrink down farther behind the bush.

"I've asked Xuegeng about his friend," said Father. "He told me that the Liangs used to serve the imperial household. They've been living in retirement after the revolution, and Baoshu's father is primarily known as a collector of old paintings."

After a moment, Mother said, "Well, that sounds harmless enough. I suppose the family must be well-to-do. Perhaps we should find a matchmaker to set things in motion. I still think it's indecent for the young people to meet like this before a formal arrangement." She added after a moment, "Even in these changing times."

Their voices faded, and I knew they were moving away. I let my breath out in a great whoosh. Things were going much too fast for me. I was concentrating on finishing school with good grades, so that I could go to medical school someday and become a doctor. Now it seemed that my parents were already talking about my marriage!

And yet I couldn't help feeling a spurt of happiness at the thought. My brothers were following the old ways in having their marriages arranged by match-makers, and they would eventually marry girls they had never seen before or had only met briefly. I would be different. I would marry someone I knew and ad-mired, someone I found exciting. I wanted to run around the courtyard and dance with joy.

If only I had someone I could talk to! I had no sisters, which Mother thought was a tremendously lucky thing. My parents wouldn't have to spend a lot of money marrying us off. But I was very lonely some-times. I had few friends in school, since most of the girls in my class considered me to be noisy and unlady-like. At times like these I really missed Tao Ailin, my only true friend.

She had sent me a couple of letters from America. One of them was about housework, of all things.

Dear Yanyan,

I've been working so hard that I don't even have time to feel lonely in this strange new country. Besides taking care of the two children, I have to help Mrs. Warner with housework and cooking. Imagine me, cooking! The first time I boiled rice, I put in so much water that it turned out as soup. Then I tried to sweep the floor, but I didn't realize that I had to gather the dirt and put it into something called a dustpan.

But I'm learning. I actually enjoy cooking!
Your friend, Ailin

I wrote back immediately.

Dear Ailin,

The most exciting thing that happened to me after seeing you off was our adventure with some hoodlums who attacked us in a Shanghai alley. My brother and his friend managed to fight them off. I think they even enjoyed the encounter. I certainly did!
Your friend, Yanyan

I didn't write to Ailin about Liang Baoshu because I wasn't sure about what to say. In another one of her letters, Ailin talked about Chinatown, an area in San Francisco that had many Chinese residents and shops. I was so startled that I wrote back immediately.

Dear Ailin,

Do you mean to say that there are parts of San Francisco under Chinese control, like the areas of Shanghai that are under British, French, and Japanese control?
Yanyan

Dear Yanyan,

No, no! Chinatown is not under Chinese control. It's called that because so many people of Chinese descent live there. I have a friend in Chinatown I often visit.

Yours, Ailin

This was the first time I learned about Ailin's friend in San Francisco. I felt a touch of jealousy. Her letters became less frequent, and I began to wonder if it was because she was spending so much time with her new friend. How could she have forgotten me so easily?

I finally learned the truth from Miss Gilbertson. In my English class the next day, I asked her if she had heard from Ailin or her employers. The Warners had planned to stay in America for a year and then return to their missionary work in China. Now that the year was almost up, I was looking forward to Ailin's returning home with them. The teacher looked at me silently for a moment. "I had a letter from the Warners," she said finally. "They write that Ailin is not coming back with them but is staying on in America. She's getting married to a man in San Francisco!"

The news left me stunned. "Who—who is the man she's marrying?" I asked when I found my voice again.

"A Chinese man she met on the ship going over. The Warners say that he's quite a decent person. Apparently he's opening a restaurant in San Francisco, and Ailin is going to help him run it."

So that was the friend in Chinatown Ailin had been talking about! For a moment I felt a sense of betrayal. When Ailin and I were in school together, we had talked about what we planned to do after graduation. I was going to be a doctor, and Ailin a teacher. Neither of us had plans to get married, and we were going to support ourselves with our earnings.

Then I remembered that I had no right to condemn Ailin. After all, I had been thinking about marriage myself, to Liang Baoshu. And in Ailin's case, becoming a teacher was no longer an option.

Still, I couldn't picture Ailin helping to run a restaurant. "Does her family know?" I asked Miss Gilbertson.

The teacher shook her head and sighed. "I don't think Ailin has been communicating with them."

I went home in a daze. I knew that Ailin's future had been profoundly changed by her refusal to have her feet bound and having her engagement broken. But I had never expected her life to take such a drastic turn. It was hard enough working as a nanny and helping out with some housework. Running a restaurant with her future husband sounded like backbreaking work.

* * *

Learning that Ailin was getting married made me think more seriously about my future with Liang Baoshu. What if he didn't like me as much as I thought he did? Not that it would make a real difference if his parents and mine were determined on the match.

But what about my ambition to become a doctor? Could a married woman work outside the home? The women teachers at the MacIntosh School, such as Miss Gilbertson and Miss Scott, were single. I had not met a married woman doctor, either. Ailin could no longer choose to train as a teacher, but I still had a choice.

As graduation time approached, I had to think more and more about my future. Several of my classmates at the MacIntosh School announced that they were getting married as soon as they graduated. A number of others said that they were getting engaged, with the wedding date still in the future. Nobody asked me about my marriage plans. I didn't have any close friends that I could talk to about personal things. Besides, I had already declared publicly that I wasn't going to get married, but planned to support myself as a doctor.

I graduated with top honors in all the science courses, but did less well in literature and calligraphy. My writing teacher told me I was too impatient and too impulsive to acquire a fine hand in brush writing. Surprisingly, I got good grades in English, which had never been one of my strong subjects.

Father asked me where I wanted to study. First I had to take premed courses, that is, subjects I had to know before I could be admitted to a medical school.

"How about one of the universities?" I asked. I remembered my brothers discussing this new type of academy. "Do they accept girls?"

"Some do," said Father. "With your grades in the sciences, I think you should be able to get in." Then he frowned. "Most of the universities are in Beijing, but things are too unsettled up there in the north. I don't like the idea of your attending school there."

It was not just the north that was unsettled. Even though our country had been a republic for ten years, we could not count on security. Here in Nanjing things were quieter, but violent outbreaks were not unknown.

At dinner that night, the unsettled condition of the country was the principal topic of conversation once more. "If only we could have the good old days again," sighed Second Brother, "when there was law and order."

"What good old days?" I demanded. "You mean the time of your hero, Confucius? He lived during a period of endless civil wars!"

"I just want a strong hand to put down all these disorders," protested Second Brother.

"Well, a strong hand did unite the country and put down disorders," Father said, and smiled.

"You mean Qin Shihuang, don't you?" I said. I turned and grinned at Second Brother. "It's true that he united the country and became the first emperor, but he was also the one who burned all those books and buried scholars alive."

Liang Baoshu was dining with us again, and Father turned to him. "What do you think? Is there someone strong enough who could unite China once again?"

"Since Yuan Shikai died," said Liang Baoshu, "a strong man hasn't appeared on the scene."

After the end of the Manchu dynasty, Yuan Shikai, a military man, became a virtual dictator and nearly succeeded in making himself emperor. Although he had died five years ago, his name still cast a shadow. Would there be another Yuan Shikai eventually?

"It's a pity that Sun Yat-sen can't remain as president," said Father. "I hear his health isn't too good."

Father was a great admirer of Sun Yat-sen, sometimes called the Father of the Republic and the man chiefly credited with bringing about the revolution ten years ago.

"The trouble with a republic is that there is no good way to determine succession," murmured Liang Baoshu. "That means there will always be a period of disorder when the president steps down."

"Then the alternative is a monarchy," said Eldest

Brother, "where you have a king automatically succeeded by his eldest son."

"Well, Britain has a monarchy, and the country seems stable enough," admitted Father. "But what if the successor is an idiot or a madman? Didn't King George the Third go mad?"

The conversation turned toward Britain, and Father began to tell stories about some of his experiences there. He described how, during a state dinner, he picked up his finger bowl and drank the water that was intended for rinsing his hands. I had heard the story before, because he told it often. Sometimes I suspected that he still smarted over the incident but thought that by telling the story over and over again, he could relieve the sting. I wondered what it felt like to live in a country where, at any moment, you could commit an embarrassing error in public.

When Liang Baoshu left that night, I still didn't know what he felt was the right form of government for China. A week later, I found out.

●　●　●

It was summer, and we spent a lot of time sitting outdoors after dinner. To repel mosquitoes, we would light an incense coil made of pressed chrysanthemums. Years later, the smell of this coil would instantly bring back memories of what happened that summer evening.

Even in our courtyard, which was near the center of our family compound, we heard shouts coming down our street. "Another riot?" said Father. "We haven't had one lately. I thought things were settling down at last."

Mother fanned herself and sighed. "When will these riots ever end? At least it's not as bad here as in the north."

Suddenly some shots rang out. I immediately thought of the shot I had heard in the Shanghai alley. That one had gone off at close quarters and left me deafened, whereas these sounded like the distant pops of firecrackers. Then some more shots went off, and they were closer. We also heard the sound of running feet.

Father got up. "I'd better tell Lao Feng to keep the front gate closed and not let anyone in."

Lao Feng was our gatekeeper, and had been working for our family since Grandfather's time. He was getting old, but Father didn't have the heart to tell him it was time to retire.

Eldest Brother emerged from his room and came over to us. "What's happening? I heard shots."

Father came back with some information. "I've been asking Lao Feng whether he heard anything. He said he asked the gatekeeper at the Li residence across the street. He told Lao Feng that the shots were fired by a troop of soldiers. It seems they were trying to arrest somebody."

The voices and the footsteps died away. It seemed that the chase had moved to another part of the city. Eldest Brother returned to his study. Mother got up from her stool and yawned. "This heat makes me tired. I think I'll go to bed a little earlier tonight."

I got up, too. I wasn't sleepy and there was still plenty of daylight left, but the mosquitoes were getting fierce and I decided to get under the mosquito net in my room. Just as I approached my door, I heard a whisper behind me. "Young Mistress, somebody wants to see you."

I turned around and saw that it was Lumei, one of our maids. "He doesn't want anyone else to know," she said. "Can you follow me?"

With my heart pounding, I followed the maid, walking as quietly as I could. We passed through two courtyards and arrived at a clump of miniature wax plum trees beside our fishpond. There was someone sitting on the ground, leaning against one of our ornamental rocks.

It was Liang Baoshu, and he was bleeding from one shoulder.

CHAPTER 4

The gunshots. The running feet. Of course. "Were you the one the police were chasing?" I asked.

He tried to smile. "Yes. I leaped over your wall. That just about finished my reserves of energy, I'm afraid."

I looked around. There was nobody else in sight, except Lumei the maid. "I won't tell anyone," she said earnestly. I could tell that to her this seemed like an exciting adventure, with Liang Baoshu as the hero. Did she see me as the heroine—or herself? For a moment I even felt a twinge of jealousy.

Then I shook myself impatiently. This was no time for romantic mooning. "How badly hurt are you?" I asked, trying to sound calm.

"One of the bullets hit me in the shoulder," replied

Liang Baoshu. After a moment he managed another smile. "You want to be a doctor. This may be your chance to practice."

I took a deep breath. "I'd better take a look."

"It seems that I'll be your first patient, Yanyan," he said.

What I noticed more than anything else was that he was addressing me by my first name—my nickname, in fact. In the last few minutes, our relationship had entered a new stage.

"Can you sit up a little, Baoshu?" I said, using his first name. "I have to look at your back to see whether the bullet passed through your shoulder or . . ." I stopped and swallowed.

"Or whether it's still inside?" he finished the sentence. With the help of the maid, he managed to sit up. From the sweat on his forehead, I could see how much the effort cost him. I unbuttoned his cloth jacket and saw the ugly hole where the bullet had gone in. Then I looked at his back.

There was no exit hole.

"I'll have to dig the bullet out," I said. I was proud of the fact that my voice wobbled only a little.

I had no time to lose, for I had to act while there was still enough light. "Get me a kitchen knife with the sharpest point you can find," I said to Lumei. "And also a bottle of our strongest *wujiapi*."

It had been five years since one of our maids had cut her hand and Father had poured the strong liquor over the wound. I had since learned that the effect of the alcohol in the liquor was to kill germs and prevent the wound from being infected. Already I had used the liquor many times to wipe the area around a wound. This time I would also have to use it to clean the kitchen knife.

Lumei hesitated only a moment before running off to obey my orders. I knew that by adopting a firm tone, I gave the impression that I knew what I was doing.

The maid returned with a truly wicked-looking knife and a small clay bottle of the liquor. Suddenly I realized that I had never handled a kitchen knife before. Well, at least I knew which was the working end: the one with the sharp point.

I poured some liquor over the knife and wiped it dry. "This is going to hurt a bit, Baoshu," I said.

"I know it will," he replied. That was the last thing he said for quite a while.

Later, what I remembered most about that probing of the wound was the sweat—or perhaps tears—streaming down my face. I had to keep wiping my eyes, and since my hands were covered with blood, I managed to smear my face.

Baoshu did not cry out. The noise would attract

attention. But I could feel his tension as he tried to keep quiet. Suddenly he relaxed.

"Is he dead?" hissed Lumei, who was helping to hold Baoshu steady.

"No, I think he's fainted," I gasped. "This is going to make things easier."

It did. For one thing, with Baoshu's muscles relaxed, I could probe more deeply. At long last, my knife hit something hard and metallic. I clenched my teeth and dug. After what seemed like years, I managed to pry the bullet out.

Looking at the small, bloody lump in my hands, I felt great sobs of relief welling up in my throat. But I couldn't afford to cry; I wasn't finished. I took the strips of cloth Lumei had brought, and the two of us did our best to bind up the wound.

During the process, Baoshu came around and began to groan. I had to put my hand over his mouth. He stared at me for a second and then nodded, to show that he understood.

It was fully dark by the time we finished. "We can't leave you out here," I said to Baoshu. "Can you walk?"

"I shall have to," he said grimly.

"We'll try to move you to that storage shed just behind the plum trees," I told him.

The maid and I succeeded in getting Baoshu to his feet. We were almost carrying him by the time we reached the storage shed. The place was bare and dusty, but it provided shelter, at least, and it was far enough away from the sleeping rooms of the family and servants so that the noises we made wouldn't attract attention. We moved some boxes and cleared a space on the floor.

"Not exactly the Great Southern Hotel, is it?" I said.

"I've slept in worse places," said Baoshu, and dropped to the floor.

The maid and I looked down at him. "We'd better let him rest," I said finally. I had no idea what to do next for someone with a hole in his shoulder. Did one administer a hot drink? Elevate his feet?

"I'll get some quilts and bedding," said Lumei. She hesitated for a moment. "Young Mistress, you'd better wash yourself. There's blood all over your face and hands."

For the first time I realized that my hands were not only sticky but reeked of blood. A wave of nausea swept over me. I took a deep breath and steadied myself. If I wanted to be a doctor, I might have to face this kind of trial again and again.

"All right," I told the maid. "Find some covers for him, and I'll try to come back later in the night."

I was wiping my face dry when I heard the pounding on our front gate. It was thunderous, loud enough for me to hear it deep inside our compound, where my sleeping room was. My heart began to beat fast. Was it possible that the police had seen Baoshu climb over our walls?

I had just changed into clean clothes and combed my hair when I heard Mother's voice. "Yanyan, are you asleep yet?"

I opened the door to my room. "No, Mother, I've been reading. What's happened? I heard the knocking at the gate."

"Father wants all of us in his study," said Mother. "The chief of police is here, and wants to know if any of us has seen an escaped criminal."

My feelings were mixed. I was relieved that there was no mention of Baoshu's name, which meant the police didn't know the identity of the fugitive they were chasing. What was worrying was why the police had come to *our* house. Had one of the other servants seen Baoshu climbing over into our compound?

When Mother and I reached Father's study, I saw that my brothers were already there. Seated next to Father was a gray-haired man who looked faintly familiar. I realized that he had visited us on social occasions. He didn't look at all threatening.

"I know that this is an unpardonable intrusion," the police chief said to Father. "The reason I came tonight is that we are chasing a dangerous plotter. According to one of my men, he was last seen running down your street. But he turned a corner, and by the time our men followed him around it, he had disappeared. Since this happened in your neighborhood, we're questioning all the households here, in case you've heard anything."

We looked at each other, but none of us spoke. "Have any of you seen or heard anything?" asked Father, looking around at us.

"We heard shouts and people running earlier," Eldest Brother said finally. "We also heard some shots."

"That was my men," said the chief of police impatiently. He waited, but no one added anything. "It's very strange, how he just disappeared into thin air."

"I suppose he could have climbed a wall," said Father.

The chief shook his head. "I don't see how. It would have taken him several minutes to climb a wall, and my men were too close on his heels."

I suddenly thought of something. Someone trained in the martial arts could have made a great leap and reached the top of the wall instantly. Did the chief of police think of this? Apparently he didn't.

But someone else did. I saw Eldest Brother stiffen. His eyes met mine, and he opened his mouth to speak. Then he closed it without saying anything.

"Tell me about your fugitive," said Father. "Is he a member of a criminal gang?"

"He belongs to a secret society that's plotting to restore the Manchu dynasty," said the chief of police. "One of our men managed to infiltrate the group, and he was the one who reported that their plans were coming to a head."

"Does your man know the identities of the plotters?" asked Eldest Brother. I held my breath as I waited for the answer to the question.

The chief shook his head. "Unfortunately, the members all wear masks, a rather melodramatic touch, but it prevented us from learning the names of the plotters. We knew the time and place of the meetings, however, and we caught some half dozen of the plotters." He rose and apologized again. "I'm sorry to intrude, and so late at night, too. But if any of you hear anything, please let me know."

After the chief of police left, the rest of us began to go to our rooms. I found myself walking next to Eldest Brother. "Someone who has connections with the Manchus . . . someone who can make a leap to the top of a wall . . . ," he murmured thoughtfully. "You realize, of course, that he could very well be inside our compound somewhere." He glanced at me.

Eldest Brother suspected something! I came to a decision. There was no way that I could safely smuggle Baoshu out without help. Eldest Brother was the person most likely to give us support, even if he was not in favor of Baoshu's plot. The two of them were close friends.

I went with Eldest Brother to his room and made sure there was no one else within earshot. "As you've guessed, Baoshu is here," I said quietly. "He's been shot, and right now he's in one of the storage sheds behind the plum trees by the pond."

Eldest Brother looked at me gravely for a long moment. "I see. And how did you happen to get involved?"

I told him about the maid. "She was the one who found him near the base of the wall, and he persuaded her to send a message to me."

Again he subjected me to a long, grave stare. "It's interesting that he should get in touch with *you* first. I notice you're calling him by his first name. Have you two been meeting secretly?"

"Of course not!" I protested. "It's just that . . . well, it seems silly to stay so formal under the circumstances."

Eldest Brother sat in thought, while I tried not to squirm. Finally he looked up at me. "Father will have to be told."

"But—but—you know what will happen!" I said. "He will tell the chief of police, and then Baoshu will be arrested!"

He looked hard at me. "Will that make you very unhappy?"

"Of course it will!" I said. "Do you mean to tell me that it won't make *you* unhappy? After all, he's your friend!"

"I *thought* he was my friend," said Eldest Brother, with a twisted smile. "But apparently we weren't friends enough for him to confide in me completely. I suspected he was involved in something, but not a conspiracy to overthrow our government!"

I had no way to stop him from telling Father. Besides, Baoshu's presence would be impossible to keep secret, anyway.

Still, I was unprepared for Father's anger. "How could I have been so blind!" he exclaimed. "To think that I was taken in by his fine talk of old-fashioned virtues! And all this time he was plotting against the government! Worst of all, he sneaked into my home and tried to corrupt my daughter!"

I wanted to protest, but my throat was too tight. It was Eldest Brother who was moved to speak. "Father, I don't think he came here meaning to corrupt Yanyan. He only saw her as someone likely to help him."

Father turned and glared at me. "And why does he think that you would be willing to help him?" Then Father asked me the same thing that Eldest Brother had. "Have you been meeting him secretly?"

"No, Father," I managed to say in a steady voice.

Father looked at me for a long moment. He knew me better than anyone, and he seemed satisfied that I was telling him the truth. "Very well. Let us go and have a look at the traitor."

Although we had installed electric lights in our living quarters, the storage shed had not been connected to an outlet, and Father carried a kerosene lamp with him to light our way. When he pushed open the door of the shed, there was an immediate rustle.

I saw Baoshu trying to sit up. He blinked in the yellow light of the lantern, and with his hair matted by perspiration and his face lined with strain, he did not look very dangerous.

"Can you give me one good reason why I should not inform the chief of police and have you instantly arrested?" Father demanded.

Baoshu tried to smile. "Because it's too late to get the chief of police out of bed?"

Father almost softened, but stiffened again when he glanced at me. "Your traitorous activity I can almost understand, given your belief in the monarchy," Father told Baoshu. "But you've put my daughter in danger by involving her. Of all the people in this household, why did you pick her to help you?"

After the barest pause, Baoshu replied, "Of all the

people in this household, she is the one who is the most ready to face danger."

Despite myself, I felt a rush of pride. Courage was what I admired most, and courage was what Baoshu thought I possessed.

Father stood silent. Finally he sighed. "Very well. I won't report you to the police. But as soon as you are well enough to move, I want you to leave us and never come here again."

● ● ●

It was impossible to keep Baoshu's presence a secret, but our servants were completely loyal, and a week passed without anyone reporting to the police. Lumei, who had found Baoshu first, attended to most of his needs, but I knew that some of the other servants also brought food and necessities.

I was forbidden by Father to go to the storage shed. After two days of anxious waiting, I went to Father and argued that if I wanted to be a doctor, I had a duty to see my patient. Father finally permitted me to see Baoshu, accompanied by Eldest Brother.

Although he had been weakened by loss of blood, Baoshu had a strong constitution, and we found him looking much improved. He was sitting propped up against some boxes and sipping a bowl of rice gruel.

He broke into a wide smile when we entered. "The wound looks to be healing nicely, and there's no sign of infection," he told me. "Your first job as a doctor seems to be a success!"

"Since you're much stronger," Eldest Brother said to Baoshu, "you should be thinking about leaving here."

I was surprised at Eldest Brother's cold tone. He and Baoshu had been close friends, after all. Had he been so shocked by the plot to restore the emperor? Then I had another thought: Maybe Eldest Brother was angry because Baoshu had said that *I* was the one in the family most ready to face danger.

Baoshu's smile faded. "Of course. I must not endanger your family any longer. I will leave as soon as I contact one of my friends to help me escape from the city."

The contact was made two days later. I didn't know how Baoshu managed to smuggle a message out, but I suspected that Lumei must have helped.

I found out about it during dinner that night. Father helped himself to a spoonful of soup, and when he had swallowed, he cleared his throat. "It seems that our, er, guest has departed. Since there has been no sound of police activity, I assume that he was able to escape safely." As he said these last words, he looked sharply at me.

I did my best to keep my face impassive. My right

hand ached, and I realized I was clutching my chopsticks so hard that my knuckles were white.

For a few minutes no one spoke around the table, and we continued with our meal. The maid brought in a steamed fish, one of Father's favorites. Usually he expressed his appreciation to the cook for preparing this difficult dish, but tonight he barely glanced at it.

I had no appetite and found it hard even to swallow, but I made a pretense of picking at my food. At last the interminable meal ended, and I was able to leave the table.

At the door to my room, I saw Lumei. Her furtive manner reminded me of the first time she had brought me a message from Baoshu. This time she was bringing another message from him, only it was a written one. "Can you find some way to meet me tomorrow afternoon near the entrance to the MacIntosh School?"

CHAPTER 5

After I read the note, I looked at Lumei. "Do you know what's in here?"

"I can't read, Young Mistress," she said. Her eyes were lowered as she replied, but I thought she sounded somewhat surly. Perhaps she resented the fact that she was illiterate.

Finding an excuse to visit the MacIntosh School was not too difficult. After my graduation, my parents and I had had many discussion about where I should attend college in order to prepare myself for a medical career. The teachers at MacIntosh had told my parents that they would be glad to write letters of recommendation for me.

When I told Mother about my wish to visit one of

the teachers of the school, she agreed readily. She was probably relieved to think that I was occupying myself with something other than Baoshu's affairs. She did insist, however, that I take the family rickshaw.

When I arrived at the school, there was a row of rickshaws in front of the gate. I got out and told our rickshaw man that since I might take a long time, he could spend some time at the tea shop around the corner. It was a place patronized by many of the other rickshaw men, and he was only too happy to go.

After he went off, I looked around, wondering what I should do next. If I just stood in front of the gate, I'd look conspicuous.

One of the other rickshaw men approached. As he drew close, he raised his straw hat just enough to expose part of his face. It was Baoshu. "Would you like a ride, Young Miss?" he asked.

Trying to look nonchalant, I nodded and got into the carriage. Was he in any condition to pull the rickshaw?

He was able to pull it down the street and around a corner, at least. As soon as we were out of sight of the other rickshaw drivers, he stopped and leaned against the side of the carriage. "We can talk here."

"Where are you staying?" I asked. "Is it a safe place?"

"Maybe it's best if I don't tell you more than you need to know," he said, and then stiffened.

I followed Baoshu's glance and saw that a policeman

was walking down the street toward us. He seemed casual enough as he glanced around. I didn't think he noticed anything particularly suspicious. He was probably just on a regular patrol.

When the policeman came up to us, I tried my best to avoid looking furtive. I had to come up with an explanation of what my rickshaw was doing stopped in the middle of the street. The best thing was to confront the enemy. "Officer, I wonder if you can help me," I said to the policeman in my best prim-young-lady voice. "I'm looking for the MacIntosh School. I know it's around here somewhere."

The policeman nodded politely to me. "It's not far, Young Miss. In fact, you just go to the end of the street and turn right at that corner there." He turned and scowled at Baoshu. "You'd think any competent rickshaw man would know the place."

"I wanted to turn there," whined Baoshu. "But the young lady kept changing her mind about which way we should go!"

"Don't pay the fellow until he gets you right to the gate of the school," advised the policeman, and walked on.

After he was out of sight, Baoshu turned and grinned at me. "That was pretty good, your helpless female act. I know how much it goes against your nature."

"Your incompetent-rickshaw-man act wasn't bad, either," I retorted. I was impressed by how well we had done in deceiving the policeman. The idea was both exciting and disquieting.

Baoshu stopped grinning. Suddenly he leaned closer and looked into my eyes. "I'm leaving Nanjing for Manchuria the day after tomorrow. Will you come away with me? I want you, Yanyan!"

I just stared at him. My heart was pounding, and even if I had had the words, I was unable to speak. "What are you saying?" I finally managed to croak.

"You must know how much you mean to me!" he whispered urgently. "Come with me to the north. Since that day in the Shanghai alley, I can't stop thinking about you, about your coolness and your bravery. I can't get you out of my mind!"

"But—but—your plans," I stammered. "I'll be in your way! You're involved in a plot to restore the monarchy. What will your friends think if I'm tagging along?"

"It doesn't matter what they think!" His eyes were bright. "What a glorious team we would make! You've always wanted adventure, Yanyan. Here is your chance!"

Things were going too fast for me. "What about my medical studies?" I asked. "I want to study to be a doctor."

"You'll get your chance to study medicine someday," he said.

"I can't decide so fast!" I protested. "I need time to think."

"You have to decide by tomorrow," he said. "Look, somebody else is coming. I'll take you back to the school."

As he set me down at the gate of the MacIntosh School, he said quietly, "Send me word by your maid. I think her name is Lumei."

"I think Lumei admires you," I said before I could stop myself.

"She's been helpful," he said impatiently. "*You're* the only one who matters to me."

I watched him go down the street and then sat down to wait for my own rickshaw man. For some reason I thought of Lumei again. She didn't matter to Baoshu. She had been simply helpful.

•   •   •

My parents could tell that something urgent was on my mind. "Have the teachers been helpful about which college you should apply for?" asked Father.

For a moment I didn't know what he was talking about. "What? Apply for college?"

Father studied my face thoughtfully. "You're still thinking about Liang Baoshu, aren't you?"

It would arouse Father's suspicion even more for me to deny it. "Can you blame me?" I muttered. "His visit here was pretty dramatic."

"You know, I've been thinking about your choice of colleges," Father said slowly. "Your English has improved a great deal, and according to your teachers the grades of your other courses are most impressive. How would you like to attend a college in England or America?"

For the second time that day, I was rendered speechless. I just gaped at him.

Father laughed. "You look like one of the fish in our carp pond, opening and closing your mouth like that!"

Suddenly, I thought of that American man we had met in our train compartment on the way to Shanghai. His response to our rude remarks about Westerners had been humorous and generous. I remembered that he had given us his name card, which said he was a professor at some college in America. Perhaps I could still find his card. It might be pleasant to attend his school.

Then the whole idea came crashing down. Baoshu! If I went with him to Manchuria, I might have to give up my plans to go to college and study medicine.

"Well?" asked Father. He was looking hard at me, and he was no longer laughing. "What do you say?"

"I need time to think," I said. "I can't decide so fast." Then I realized that I had said that earlier, too.

That night I couldn't sleep as I tried to make up my mind. If I went with Baoshu, I would very likely have to give up my plans to become a doctor. He had said that I could still study medicine someday, but when would that opportunity come, if ever? I might have to travel from place to place with him, dodging the police, eluding capture.

But what an adventure it would be, the two of us working together and braving dangers! Baoshu could teach me more martial arts, and I would realize my dream of becoming one of those women warriors I was always reading about. I might even help with the wounded if one of the conspirators got hurt. Again I felt a rush of pride as I remembered how I had dug the bullet from Baoshu's shoulder.

With the pride, however, I felt a keen regret. If I gave up going to medical school, my practice would never go beyond digging out bullets.

Studying in America, that would also be a great adventure! I thought of my friend, Tao Ailin, and her experiences in the city called San Francisco. Her life sounded hard, but so exciting that I almost writhed with envy as I read her letters.

Going to America meant giving up Baoshu. I remembered his eyes as he begged me to go with him, and my throat tightened painfully at the thought of never seeing him again.

Then I remembered something else: the careless way he had talked about Lumei, who had helped him and admired him so much. What if he became tired of me? Would he talk about me in the same careless way?

I tossed and turned most of the night. Sometime in the early hours of the morning, I must have fallen asleep. When I opened my eyes, the sun was already up. I struggled from my bed, and as I blearily looked around for my clothes, I realized that I still hadn't made up my mind. In the course of this day, I would have to tell Baoshu my decision.

That morning, it was as if my thinking about Ailin had produced immediate results. As we finished eating and got up from the table, Mother suddenly turned to me. "Oh, I almost forgot. Yesterday a letter arrived for you from your friend, Tao Ailin."

She went to a small cupboard, took out the letter, and handed it to me. I tore open the envelope.

Dear Yanyan,

You've probably heard already from Miss Gilbertson that I'm not returning to China with the Warners. I've decided to marry a man called James Chew. He plans to open a restaurant in Chinatown here in San Francisco, and I'm going to help him run it.

I expect my life to be pretty hard, especially for the next couple of years, but I'm fully prepared for it.

I don't see how I can face the sort of life an upper-class Chinese woman would lead. Spending all day playing mahjong and gossiping with friends would drive me crazy.

In the restaurant I'll have to wash dishes and chop vegetables, but at least I know that I'll be playing an essential role in making the restaurant a success. Self-respect is what I value more than anything else.

Self-respect. That was something I valued too. It was something Father had instilled in me. He was unlike most Chinese fathers in this, since self-respect was not a trait encouraged in girls. Could I maintain it if I became Baoshu's helper and accomplice? I would not be fighting for a cause I believed in. I would be acting only to please Baoshu.

At the end of the letter, Ailin said,

I feel that my father would have approved of what I'm doing, even though washing dishes in a restaurant is not considered a respectable occupation for a young lady in China.

*Please don't despise me for choosing this path. I hope
we can remain friends.*

Ailin

Ailin's mention of her father's approval hit me like
a physical blow. One thing I had failed to consider in
trying to make up my mind was how my decision would
affect Father. He had been so proud of me for wanting
to become a doctor. I remembered how much pleasure
he had taken in showing me germs with his microscope.

How would he feel if I gave up my ambition to study
medicine? Even worse, I would be joining someone
who was plotting to restore the Manchu dynasty and
destroy the republic. Father would be hurt beyond
measure. It would be like thrusting a knife into his
heart.

I heard Mother's voice. "What does Ailin's letter
say?"

"Sh-she said she and her husband are planning to
open a restaurant," I replied. "She will have to work
v-very h-hard, she said."

Suddenly I realized that tears were streaming down
my face. Muffling my sobs with my sleeve, I ran to
my room. I flung myself on my bed and cried and
cried, until my throat was scraped raw by my harsh
sobs.

"Are you all right?" asked Mother. She stood at the

door, her eyes wide with worry. "Is it something in Ailin's letter? Is she very unhappy?"

I had forgotten that Mother, too, would be heartbroken if I ran away with Baoshu. I sat up and mopped my eyes. My decision was made.

"No, Ailin is not unhappy at all," I told Mother. "In fact, I would like to go to America and see her."

After Mother made a few soothing noises and left my room, I took out my pen and a piece of paper. My message to Baoshu was short. It said, "I'm sorry. I cannot go with you."

Lumei took my message, and within an hour she returned with Baoshu's answer. His message was even shorter than mine. "I'm not giving up," it said.

●　●　●

"Cornell?" said Father. "I've heard of the college, I think. Whatever made you choose that one? It's in a small town, far away from any big city."

I showed him the calling card from the man I had met on the train. "We met this man on the way to Shanghai. He's a professor at Cornell University, and he seems to be a very nice person. So if I have any problems, I can always go to him for help."

Father read the card. "Hmm . . . George Pettigrew, professor of Oriental history."

"He also speaks very good Chinese," I added. I didn't

tell him about the embarrassing circumstances in which I had found out that Professor Pettigrew spoke good Chinese.

"Very well," said Father. "Let me make some inquiries about Cornell. The teachers in your school might be able to give us some advice, too."

Father liked what he learned about Cornell University. Unlike some of the other famous American universities, it was not connected to any religious organization. What he liked best was that it had been coeducational from its very beginning. It seemed that the founder of the university, Ezra Cornell, believed strongly in a good education for women.

"Yanyan might get unladylike ideas at such a school," protested Mother. "Not that she doesn't have enough of them already! Can't we send her to a girls' college? She would get an education suitable for a well-bred young lady."

Father glanced at me, and there was both pride and a touch of despair in his eyes. "I think making Yanyan into a well-bred young lady is a hopeless cause, anyway. She has stated that she wants to be a doctor, and I hear that Cornell has a good medical program. I'm going to write to the university and see if she can be admitted there. It is already summer, very late in the year to apply for admittance, but exceptions may be made for a special case like hers."

During the days that followed, I found it hard to hide my nervousness. My parents thought I was worried about being admitted to Cornell. I didn't tell them that I had something else on my mind as well.

Baoshu's message didn't say what he was planning to do. It was possible that he was too busy trying to escape from the city to think about me. Or perhaps he had already left Nanjing and was now safe in Manchuria. I watched Lumei anxiously to see if she had another message for me.

Finally I was driven to ask her if she had heard from Baoshu. "No," she said curtly. "I would have told you immediately if I had word."

Father finally received an answer from the Cornell admissions office. "They said they will let you enroll as a special student for the coming semester," he told me. "If you do well, you will be admitted as a regular fresh-man in the spring."

In the next few weeks I was swept up in a whirlwind of activity and became almost too busy to fret over Baoshu. Mother hired a seamstress to make Western-style clothes for me. When I was a young child, I was dressed in traditional Chinese clothes for young girls, consisting of trousers and a tunic that buttoned down the side, Manchu-style. Except for differing materials, it was what most women wore. After the revolution, many of the younger women adopted styles that were partly influenced by the West. They wore long skirts, with the Manchu tunic on top. Schoolgirls like me wore shorter skirts that were midcalf in length, with the same sort of tunic.

But now I was having clothes made that looked like those worn by my American teachers at the MacIntosh School. Instead of tunics, I had blouses that buttoned down the front, with a heavier jacket worn over the blouse. What I found hardest to get used to was the material of the jackets and skirts, which were mostly made of wool. Woolen clothing was warm, and this was necessary according to Father, because I would be going to a place where the winters were bitterly cold. But I found the wool scratchy, and wondered how my teachers could stand wearing this material day after day. Maybe that was why Miss Scott was always so ill-tempered.

A big problem was finding someone to accompany me on the long journey. Mother was horrified when she found out that after crossing the Pacific, I still had to travel almost the whole width of America to reach the town where Cornell was situated. "It's unthinkable for a respectable young girl like Yanyan to travel alone all that distance!" she insisted.

I suddenly thought of Professor Pettigrew again. He

had said that he and his wife would be returning to America. If they hadn't already left, I could go with them.

Father thought this was an excellent idea. "I see that you're really using your head, Yanyan! You must be very eager to go to Cornell."

He took me to call on Professor Pettigrew that very afternoon. It turned out that the Pettigrews were good friends of Miss Gilbertson. The Americans in Nanjing formed a small, tight community.

My cheeks burned slightly to see Mr. Pettigrew again, but he seemed genuinely happy that I had contacted him. And his wife was also warm and welcoming.

"You're Sheila, aren't you?" said Mrs. Pettigrew. "Frances Gilbertson told us about you."

Miss Gilbertson had given each student in her class an English name, and mine was Sheila. Ailin's English name was Eileen, which sounded pretty close. I hated my name of Sheila, but since Americans would have trouble with my Chinese name of Xueyan, I was resigned to using it.

Mrs. Pettigrew had round, pink cheeks, and when she laughed, which she did often, she showed a mouthful of very big white teeth. I was alarmed when she looked me up and down and exclaimed, "Oh, you little darling! I could just eat you up!"

What was it about me that made people think of food? I remembered that one of the hoodlums in the Shanghai alley had called me a juicy morsel. It didn't go with the image of the woman warrior I aspired to be.

When Father told the Pettigrews that I was planning to attend Cornell, it was Mrs. Pettigrew herself who suggested that I travel on the same boat with them and then take the same train across the United States.

Even Mother became reassured when she heard about my travel arrangements. One drawback of going with the Pettigrews, however, was that they had booked passage on a boat that would sail to Seattle, a city in the northwest corner of America. From Seattle, they planned to take a train that would go along a northerly route to Ithaca, New York. I had already written to Ailin to tell her I was coming to attend school in America, but now I had to tell her that my boat wouldn't be landing in San Francisco, and I wouldn't be able to visit her when I landed. I would have to find another opportunity to see her.

•   •   •

My last few days in Nanjing were filled with a frenzy of activity. When the day arrived for departure, I was so tired that I hardly felt a thing upon leaving the city that had been my home for the whole of my life.

At the Shanghai docks, I couldn't help remembering the day when I had come to see Ailin off. At that time, I had ached with envy because Ailin was embarking on a great adventure, while I had little hope of ever visiting America.

This time I was embarking for America myself. When Ailin left, I had been the only person to see her off. Today, my parents were on the docks waving good-bye to me. I saw Mother wiping her eyes with a handkerchief. I would be a grown-up young lady by the time she saw me again.

Ailin had scanned the crowd for the sight of a friendly face. I scanned the crowd too, for another face. Suddenly I thought I saw Baoshu. But it turned out to be someone else. He had sent no word at all. A sudden wave of anguish passed over me, for I didn't expect to see him again.

CHAPTER 6

*A*t the MacIntosh School I had studied the geography of America, but I was still unprepared for the real thing. Our ship docked at Seattle, where we were to spend the night before getting on the train that would take us across the continent to New York State.

The waterfront, instead of teeming with people as in Shanghai, looked almost deserted by comparison. What really startled me was the sight of some people in the streets who had brownish faces and straight black hair.

"Were those people Chinese?" I whispered to Mr. Pettigrew as we went into our hotel.

"They're Indians," said Mr. Pettigrew. "Some of them

leave their reservations and come into the city to look for work."

"I thought Indians wore feathered headdresses, lived in tents, and rode horses!" I said, shocked and disappointed. These Indians wore the same sort of cotton shirts and pants as the white men around them.

Mr. Pettigrew grinned. "You also thought Indians had red skin, remember?"

I nodded, embarrassed. It seemed that my ideas about America, obtained mostly from hearsay, were turning out to be inaccurate. At the hotel that night, I wrote home to tell my parents that I had arrived safely in America. I also wrote to Ailin.

Dear Ailin,

By now you will have received my letter saying that I was coming to America. Our ship docked in Seattle, which is in the northwest corner of the country. It's a beautiful city, surrounded by distant mountains covered with snow, even at the end of summer. I saw some real Indians! Only they didn't look the way I expected. In fact, a lot of things aren't turning out the way I expected.

Tomorrow morning we start our train trip across America. I don't expect our train to be attacked by Indians riding on horseback.

It's too bad that I won't see you before I go to the East Coast. I hope we can arrange to meet later.

Yanyan

* * *

Our train traveled across the northern part of America, and I followed our progress on a map I had with me. We started by going through the states of Washington and Idaho, which were mountainous and heavily forested at first. I had never seen so many trees before in my life! No wonder most of the houses we saw were built of wood instead of brick or mud. Not that we saw many houses. I was amazed at how empty the country was. We would go for hours and hours and not see a single town!

The land became flatter, and when we reached the state of Montana, we saw some people on horseback. "They're cowboys," Mr. Pettigrew told me. "Out here in the West they still have ranches and cowboys, although the numbers are dwindling every year."

I had read about cowboys, and they seemed like very romantic figures. For an instant I felt a pang as I remembered how Baoshu loved to ride horses. I resolutely turned my thoughts away from Baoshu. "If there are cowboys around here, shouldn't there be Indians, too? Indians on horseback with feathered headdresses?"

Mr. Pettigrew laughed. "You don't give up, do you? Actually, you may be right in that the Indians around here are the horse-riding type. The ones we saw in Seattle are very different. In that part of the country, the Indians mostly live by hunting, fishing, and gathering." His face grew somber. "At least they used to."

"So there are many different kinds of Indians, then?" I asked.

"My dear, there are as many different kinds of Indians as there are different kinds of Chinese," said Mr. Pettigrew. "The Seattle Indians are as different from New York State Indians as you are from a Mongolian."

I was reminded again that America was a vast country. We left the mountainous states of the West and passed through almost endless stretches of desertlike land before we reached the greener states of the Midwest, Minnesota and Wisconsin. It was strange to see so many acres of lush farmland with so few people living on them.

We changed trains in Chicago, the biggest city I had seen so far. From there on, we began to see more people. After so many miles of emptiness, I felt warmed by the sight of the crowds. In fact, there was comparatively little emptiness from that point on. As we proceeded farther east, we seldom lost sight of some little town or city. There would be no more cowboys or Indians on horses. Cornell was situated in Ithaca,

New York. Did that mean we would be close to the biggest city in America?

To my surprise, we changed trains at a medium-sized city and took a smaller train that went south. "Ithaca is in the central part of New York State, quite some distance from New York City," Mrs. Pettigrew told me, answering my question.

On a late summer afternoon, after a journey lasting nearly a month, I finally arrived in the town that would be my home for the next four years.

●　●　●

The first thing to do was find a place where I could rent a room. I couldn't live with the Pettigrews since their two teenaged sons would be coming home at the end of summer and their house had barely enough room for their own family.

The rooming house that the Pettigrews found for me was on a steep street not far from the campus of Cornell University. It was run by a widow, Mrs. Harte. It amazed me that in America a woman could own property, such as this huge three-story house with six bedrooms. Mrs. Harte had begun taking in boarders after her husband's death six years ago. I learned that *boarders* meant people who rented a room from her and also ate their meals with her.

When I said good-bye to the Pettigrews at the front

door of Mrs. Harte's house, it was a bit like waving farewell to my parents all over again. Mrs. Pettigrew gave me a hug that squeezed all the air out of me. "We want you to visit us often, do you hear?"

"If you have any problem whatsoever, come straight to us," Mr. Pettigrew said. "You can also see me at my office at the university."

"And remember, Sheila, you're expected for dinner this Sunday," said Mrs. Pettigrew as they left.

I had to blink away tears as I watched the Pettigrews walk out of sight. During the long journey I had been too excited to feel homesick, and besides, I knew that being on the boat and the train was only temporary. But now I realized that I was ten thousand miles away from home, and living in a strange town where I knew almost nobody. For the first time in my life, I was completely on my own.

I was so overwhelmed with loneliness that I didn't know how I could last even a week in Ithaca. The four years it would take to finish my undergraduate studies stretched like an eternity ahead of me.

I went upstairs to my room and sat down on the narrow bed, feeling too wretched even to rouse myself to unpack my things. I didn't know how long I sat there. Maybe an hour, maybe several hours. Finally there was a knock on the door. "Do you have everything you need, dear?" said Mrs. Harte's voice.

I got up and opened the door. "Yes, thank you, Mrs. Harte," I managed to say.

"Supper is at six o'clock," she told me, and handed me some towels.

After she left, I washed my face in the enamel basin in one corner of the room. I looked in the mirror above the basin, and I saw a frightened child with quivering lips.

Suddenly I gritted my teeth. To think that I prized courage more than anything else! I had once pictured myself living with Baoshu in some remote Manchurian forest, and here I was sniveling merely because I found myself in a small American town.

I opened my suitcases, grabbed my clothes, and stuffed them roughly away into drawers. It was time to get on with my life.

At supper that night, I sat down at a table with three strangers, two men and a young woman. Mrs. Harte introduced me to the others as Sheila. The man next to me said his name was Joe, and that his friend across the table was Marvin. "We work in a bank downtown," he said.

I knew that banks were places where people kept money. "What is your job at the bank?" I asked Joe.

"Tell her," he said—or I thought he said.

I glanced around at Marvin, waiting for him to tell me. But he just looked blank.

Finally Joe said slowly and distinctly, "I'm a teller. That's my job."

"Oh," I said. I wanted to know what he was supposed to tell, but I decided to wait for some future occasion to ask him.

I turned to the young woman, who smiled at me and told me her name was Sibyl. "Are you just visiting America?"

"No, I expect to stay here for four years," I said. "I'm a student, and I'm planning to attend Cornell University."

"That's great!" said Sibyl. "I'm a librarian at the univeristy. If you like, I can take you with me to the campus tomorrow morning and show you around."

I was warmed by her friendliness, and so grateful for the offer that I didn't take much notice of the food. Like the meals aboard the boat and the train, Mrs. Harte's supper was very heavy on meat. The only vegetable was a yellowish mound. I poked at it.

"It's creamed spinach," Sibyl told me. The vegetable didn't resemble anything I had eaten before, and I resolved to look up *spinach* in my Chinese-English dictionary.

* * *

When I went to bed that night, I expected homesickness to keep me awake, but I actually fell asleep fairly quickly. Next morning, however, when I awoke and saw my bleak little room, I was swept by another wave of miserable loneliness. Hearing sounds of the other roomers stirring, I forced myself out of bed and got dressed.

There was no time for self-pity. Coming to America was a great adventure, I reminded myself. Besides, I had too much to do.

First of all, I had to ask Mrs. Harte where I could find a laundress, since I was running out of clean underwear and blouses. On board the train, I had followed Mrs. Pettigrew's example and rinsed out a few things by hand, but it was time for my clothes to get a thorough laundering.

"I send my linens out to a laundry every Monday," said Mrs. Harte. "Some of my roomers also include their laundry, and you can do that, too, if you want."

This was Wednesday. Monday was five days away. "Well, I need some clean clothes right away," I said.

"Why do you need to send out your laundry, anyway?" asked Mrs. Harte. "I thought all Chinese are experts at laundering."

"What makes you think that?" I asked, puzzled.

Mrs. Harte looked a little embarrassed. "Well—that is—all the laundries in town are run by Chinamen."

I received the news with mixed feelings. It seemed that there were other Chinese in town, so I wasn't totally cut off from those of my race. But why were all the laundries run by Chinese?

Mrs. Harte tried to tell me how to get to the nearest Chinese laundry, but since I didn't know the town at all, I decided to find it later. Sighing, I rinsed out a few things again by hand.

After breakfast, my next problem was buying some pencils, notebooks, and other school supplies. Handling money was one of the things I needed to practice. In China I didn't spend money, since I never went out shopping. All my clothes, and even my shoes, were made to order for me, and everything else I needed was purchased by my parents.

On the train, Mrs. Pettigrew had showed me the different bills and coins of American money and told me the sort of things I could buy with them. Occasionally, when we had a stop that lasted for some time, I would go to the platform and practice spending some money. Of course I had no idea what to buy, so I just grabbed whatever was available that looked interesting. I usually got newspapers, magazines, and candy.

Here in Ithaca, I had to learn how to shop all by myself. Sibyl turned out to be helpful again. She told me about a store on campus where students at the university did a lot of their shopping.

We set off to the campus together. "Are we *walking*

there?" I asked when we started up a very steep street that seemed to go up almost vertically.

Sibyl looked surprised. "How else do you expect us to go?"

"Well . . . ," I faltered, "I guess you don't have rickshaws in America, do you?"

I had to explain what a rickshaw was to Sibyl. For an instant, I pictured Baoshu disguising himself as a rickshaw man.

Meanwhile Sibyl was saying that it was cruel to make another person pull you along in a two-wheeled cart. "Besides, they'd never get it up this hill!"

I had to agree with her. I was already panting hard, and we had barely begun our climb. "How do people get around in an American city, then? Do you walk everywhere?"

"Some people have automobiles," said Sibyl. She peered at me. "You do know what an automobile is, don't you?"

"Of course I do," I said. Father had talked about them, only he had called them motorcars.

"There are a few automobiles in Ithaca," said Sibyl, "but they are expensive, so not many people have them. Mind you, some people have bicycles. Only they're pretty hard to ride on a steep hill like this."

I knew what a bicycle was, having seen pictures of

some in books at the MacIntosh School. "So you walk everywhere, here in Ithaca?" I asked.

"No, you can ride omnibuses downtown," said Sibyl. "They're called buses for short, and they're like big automobiles for use by the public."

"You mean like a train, then?" I asked.

"No, trains run on tracks, and buses go on a regular street," said Sibyl. "Trolleys are more like trains, and they run on tracks."

What with trolleys, buses, and trains, I was becoming very confused. I was also getting breathless. Sibyl seemed to be very fit, and she was striding up the hill with no difficulty whatsoever. I wondered how old she was. But when I asked her what her age was, she looked offended. "It's none of your business!" she said curtly.

I was shocked. In China we often asked people how old they were, but American customs could be quite different, as I had discovered while traveling with the Pettigrews. "I'm s-sorry," I stammered. "Is it rude in America to ask people how old they are?"

Sibyl's face softened a little. "Yes, it is. You must never ask people their age, unless it's a very young child." After a moment, she said, "Okay, I don't mind telling you. I'm twenty-eight years old, and I'm still unmarried. That means I'll probably be an old maid."

It was not hard to guess what an old maid was. "I'm

going to be an old maid, too," I said eagerly. "I'm study-ing to become a doctor so I can support myself and don't have to marry anybody." For a brief moment I thought of Baoshu again, but I firmly pushed that thought away.

Sibyl smiled at me. "Long live old maids! We don't need husbands, do we?"

There was something so vigorous and independent about Sibyl that my heart lightened. Maybe America was a good place for me, if there were lots of women like her who walked everywhere and didn't have to de-pend on anyone.

We finally arrived at the campus of the university, and not a moment too soon. I had never climbed so hard before in my life, and my legs felt like overcooked noodles. "How much higher than the town is the uni-versity?" I asked.

"It's four hundred feet higher than the town proper," she told me, grinning. "Scary, isn't it? Students like you who live in town complain bitterly about having to climb so much every day, especially if they go home for lunch. But you'd be surprised how much easier it will be when you get used to it."

"If I live that long," I gasped.

Seeing that I was exhausted, Sibyl didn't take me to many places. She pointed out the administration building, where I would have to go first thing next

Monday when the university started. She also showed me Sage Hall, a dormitory for women students. If I eventually became a regular student, that was one place where I could live.

Next, we went to a small store for students. I was able to buy a few things, such as soap, handkerchiefs, and a map of the town. Sibyl's eyes widened when she saw the roll of money I took out of my handbag. "Don't take so much money around with you," she whispered to me as we left the store. "Better keep it locked up in your room."

For a moment I had a vision of the hoodlums in the Shanghai alley. "You mean you have robbers attacking people here in Ithaca?"

"No, no," she said quickly. "But there may be pickpockets."

"Pick pockets?" I asked. I didn't understand what she meant.

"Someone might pick your pocket," explained Sibyl patiently—very patiently.

I looked at the pocket of my jacket. There was nothing special about it. "Why should anyone choose my pocket?"

Sibyl rolled her eyes. I recognized that expression, because I had seen it often on the faces of my mother and Second Brother. It was time to drop the subject.

After the shopping, I was more than ready for some lunch and a rest. Sibyl had to go to work, so I made my way downhill back to Mrs. Harte's house by myself. It had been an adventurous morning. I had gone shopping at a store for the first time in my life, and I had been able to walk all alone in a strange city. Maybe this wasn't as heroic as joining Baoshu and his fellow conspirators, but I was still proud of myself.

*   *   *

The exercise gave me an appetite, and I ate Mrs. Harte's hearty lunch of macaroni and cheese. Cheese was something I usually avoided when it was served aboard the ship or the train. Like most Chinese, I didn't care much for milk. Cheese, made from *fermented* milk, sounded even worse. The dish Mrs. Harte served consisted of a big mound of chopped-up noodles cooked in a sticky, yellowish sauce. I didn't find out until afterward that the sauce was made of cheese. It wasn't all that bad.

Woozy with fatigue and heavy food, I lay down on my bed and fell asleep. I had intended to catch a brief nap, but when I woke up and looked at my bedside clock, I discovered that it was nearly four.

I got up, still a little dizzy. The room was warm, and my clothes felt sticky. Suddenly, I hated my heavy

Western clothes and longed for a loose tunic made of silk. My blouse was badly wrinkled, and the woolen skirt smelled from being worn continually for weeks. I decided to look for the laundry Mrs. Harte had mentioned earlier.

She showed me on the map where the laundry was, and I set out with my bundle of dirty clothes. I had to go downhill, and my heart sank at the prospect of having to climb back up again.

Fortunately the laundry was not far away. Compared to Nanjing and Shanghai, the only two cities I really knew, Ithaca was small and compact. I got lost only twice before I found the place. Several times, when I stopped to consult my map, passersby asked me if I needed help. I was not used to having strangers speak to me—my experience in the Shanghai alley didn't help—so I just shook my head and backed nervously away. It was several weeks before I realized that kindness to strangers was an American trait.

Finally, I found the laundry. What drew my attention to the place was not the sign in English, but the two big Chinese characters meaning "flowery stream." My eyes fastened hungrily on them the way a starving man stares at a bowl of steaming rice. I hadn't seen Chinese writing since stepping off the boat in Seattle, and that seemed like many years ago.

I took a deep breath and entered the laundry. It was a

small place and had a pleasant smell of soap. A tiny Chinese man came out. Then I realized that he was not really tiny but was actually a bit taller than I was. After so many days of seeing hefty Westerners, he only seemed small.

I put my bundle of clothes on the counter and asked him if he could wash them for me. He just stared at me. Thinking he was hard of hearing, I repeated my question, speaking slowly and distinctly. Finally he said something, and I discovered that I couldn't understand him at all.

That was when I realized that I had spoken in Mandarin and he had answered in Cantonese. The two dialects were mutually incomprehensible. I tried again, speaking English this time. "Can you wash these clothes for me?"

He finally smiled. "Yes. You need them soon?"

I nodded vigorously, greatly relieved at being able to communicate at last. "Can I have them later this week?"

"Yes," he repeated. Then he looked curiously at me. "You've just come to Ithaca, miss?"

"I came two days ago," I said. It felt like two months. Suddenly, I had an urge to ask if I could rent a room with his family. It would be like being halfway back to China. But I knew it was a ridiculous idea. The laundry looked tiny, and living quarters would be very limited.

Then another idea occurred to me. I had a sudden hunger for Chinese food. After more than a month of meat and potatoes—except for today's macaroni and cheese—I felt an overwhelming desire for rice and crunchy green vegetables. I wanted a rest from huge slabs of red meat and mushy, yellowish, unidentifiable mounds of vegetables.

"Is there a restaurant near here serving Chinese food?" I asked.

The laundry man nodded. "Yes, two blocks down the street, on the right-hand side."

Although it was only five in the afternoon, I headed for the restaurant. I felt very daring. Eating in the Shanghai hotel restaurant with Eldest Brother had seemed like an adventure at the time. Now here I was, planning to eat in a foreign restaurant all by myself! But my desperate need for Chinese food drove me on.

Again, it was the Chinese characters above the front entrance that drew my eyes. *Tao Yuan,* it said, "Peach Garden." I took a deep breath, opened the door, and went in. There were a number of small tables, but no diners. I was apparently the first customer.

A Chinese man appeared, and this time I didn't make the mistake of speaking Mandarin. "Can I have supper here?" I asked in English, trying to appear nonchalant, as if I were quite used to dining out alone.

He hesitated for just a second but did not seem scandalized. "Yes, of course," he said. He led me to a table, pulled a chair out for me, and handed me a menu.

I read the list of dishes—they were all in English—but none of the items on the menu made any sense. Finally I decided on chop suey, a dish I had never heard of before. I decided to gamble on sweet-and-sour pork, because at least I knew what pork was, although I didn't recall ever eating it sweet and sour at home. I also ordered steamed rice, which was something I knew, at least.

As my order was being prepared, several other customers came in. They were all Americans. They seemed to know what they wanted, and I was relieved to hear that their orders included chop suey and sweet-and-sour pork.

When my food came, I stared at it in amazement. Everything was on a large dinner plate, and instead of chopsticks, my utensils consisted of a knife and a fork. The rice I recognized. Next to it was finely shredded cabbage, bean sprouts, and slivers of meat, all swimming in a brown gravy. The third component consisted of cubes of meat in an orange-colored sauce. I decided to tackle the chop suey first. The vegetables were crunchy and went well with the rice. Best of all, the dish contained soy sauce. I hadn't realized how much I missed its distinctive flavor until I tasted it again, after being without it for more than a month.

When the waiter came to collect the dishes, I asked him if the food was Cantonese. He looked apologetic. "Not really. I guess you can call it Chinese-American."

I understood. Since his customers all seemed to be Americans, he had to offer them what they wanted— or what he thought they wanted.

Halfway to the kitchen, he turned back to me and whispered, "To stay in business, I have to give my American customers what they expect, you see. Next time, I can give you some real Chinese food, if you want." I was touched and whispered my thanks.

I was wrong about all the customers being Americans. As I rose to leave the restaurant, the door opened and three young Chinese came in, two boys and a girl. What riveted my attention was that they were speaking Mandarin.

One of the boys was saying, "I don't know why we have to come here! We can't afford to eat in a restaurant very often. When we do, I'd rather save my money for some better place, either in Syracuse or Rochester."

"I'm sick and tired of the food at our rooming house!" said the other boy. "Tonight's menu features corned beef and cabbage again." He turned to the girl. "Why don't you cook another dinner for us? Your last attempt wasn't at all bad."

The girl pouted. "Why do I have to do all the work?

Why don't *you*—" She stopped as she caught sight of me.

The two boys followed her glance, and I found myself being studied by three pairs of eyes. Flustered and excited at the same time, I smiled weakly at them. They just stared with their mouths open. I finally groped my way to the door and left the restaurant.

They were Chinese students, and there was a good chance I might see them again on campus! Suddenly I felt a lot less lonely.

After arriving in Ithaca, I had been too depressed even to write letters. But when I returned to my room at Mrs. Harte's house, I finally picked up my pen and pulled out my writing pad.

Dear Ailin,

Here I am in Ithaca, New York, the small town where I will be living for the next four years. The streets are very, very steep, and I got more exercise in one day than I got in four years of gym classes at the MacIntosh School.

I thought at first that I would be the only Chinese in town, but I found a Chinese laundry and even a Chinese restaurant. I missed Chinese food so much that I went in all by myself and ordered a meal! They served me some pieces of pork in a bright orange-colored sauce that was both sour and very, very sweet. Do you serve it in your restaurant, too? How about something called chop suey? Suey must come from the word meaning small pieces, and chop must be the English word for cutting things up. You'll have to teach me some basics about Chinese-American restaurant food!

I'm still hoping that we'll get a chance to meet soon.

Yanyan

CHAPTER 7

*B*efore classes began at the university, Mr. Pettigrew took me to see the student advisor to decide on what courses I should take. "Since I want to be a doctor, I should enroll in science classes," I told the advisor. "I want to take physics, chemistry, biology, and mathematics."

The advisor frowned. He was a painfully thin man with a deeply lined face. Perhaps he wasn't really frowning, and the line between his brows was permanent. Nevertheless, I could tell he wasn't pleased by my choices. "Female students generally take home economics when they enter the university," he told me.

I didn't know what home economics was, and Mr. Pettigrew had to explain. "In a home economics course, you learn the most efficient ways to cook, sew, and clean house. You also get important information on nutrition and how to promote the health of your family."

"My family's health is important, and that's why I want to study medicine," I said. "But I don't need to learn about cooking, sewing, and cleaning house. We have a chef to do the cooking, seamstresses to do the sewing, and maids to do the cleaning."

This time there was no mistaking the advisor's frown. It made a deep indentation in his brow, like a knife gash. "Here at Cornell, we teach young ladies all the womanly arts in order to make them proper wives and mothers."

"But I don't intend to——" I began.

Mr. Pettigrew interrupted me, and he spoke in Chinese. "I think it would be a good idea for you to do what he says, Sheila. If you want to be admitted as a regular student, you have to show yourself willing to take the courses that regular students take."

"You mean all the students at Cornell learn to cook and sew and clean house?" I asked.

Mr. Pettigrew laughed. "No, only the female students. You see, in America, very few families have servants. Women are more independent here, and they do most of the household tasks themselves."

His mention of independent women reminded me of Sibyl. She didn't wait for a rickshaw, but set off on foot and climbed up that steep hill to the university.

I decided to enroll in the home economics course. To be accepted as a regular student I had better do what was expected of me. For an instant, I thought of the cook at the Chinese restaurant. He made chop suey and sweet-and-sour pork because that was what his customers expected from him. Maybe he had taken a home economics course too.

Learning to cook might even be useful and fun. I was reminded of the letter I had just received from Ailin.

Dear Yanyan,

Guess what? I'm doing more than just washing dishes at our restaurant. I actually did some cooking the other evening! Our customers liked my food, especially the stir-fried pork and mushrooms. I hope you can come to our restaurant and taste some of my dishes.

Ailin

After I told my advisor that I would take the home economics course, he said I should also take a course in English. "And you should think twice about that physics course," he added. "It's usually taken by second-year students. It will be much too hard for you."

That immediately made me determined to take the course. "I'm prepared to work very hard in the physics course," I said firmly.

"Sciences such as physics are not really suited to the female mentality," said the advisor. The line between his brows became deeper and darker. "You would do better to take a foreign language. French adds an elegant gloss to a young lady's education."

"I don't need an elegant gloss," I said. Anyway, Father had said that it was hopeless trying to make me into a refined young lady.

Despite the advisor's obvious disapproval, I chose the physics course, as well as a freshman mathematics course ("Also unsuited to the female mentality," I thought I heard him mutter). But I compromised by accepting his suggestion to take the English course. I could already speak English, but there was a lot of room for improvement.

* * *

I was losing weight from all the climbing and found the waistbands of my skirts getting looser. Since childhood, I had always been a little on the plump side. Was that why people thought of food when they saw me? But when I looked in the mirror now, I saw that even my cheeks were not as round as they used to be. Mother would have a shock if she saw me, and she would insist on stuffing me with sweetmeats. I wondered what Baoshu would think of my face now.

By the time classes began, I was proud to make it up to the university campus with only a little bit of wheezing. On the first day of school, I found myself jostled on all sides by throngs of other students rushing to their classes. The MacIntosh School in Nanjing had about two hundred pupils. More than ten times that many attended Cornell. The campus was very large, and sometimes the distance between classrooms was so great that I had to dash frantically to reach my next class in time. When a thousand other students were also dashing to their next class, I had to be careful to avoid a collision. Since most of the students were much bigger than I was, I was constantly in danger of being knocked down and trampled underfoot. It was worse than trying to swim in a fast current.

Schoolwork turned out to be hard, much harder than I had expected. Since my classes at the MacIntosh School had been easy for me, I had thought that they would be easy here as well.

My home economics course turned out to be a real challenge. The lectures were not hard to follow, being mostly about things like the nutritional values of beef, mutton, dairy products, and so on. We never ate beef at home, since it was considered an inferior kind of meat, and mutton was eaten only by northerners, who didn't mind the smell. The lectures about sanitation, however, I found very interesting. The discussion of germs really made me sit up, because I recalled seeing them in Father's microscope. It seemed that some germs caused wounds to fester, while others could turn food and water poisonous.

The hard part for me was when we had to do things with our own hands. The teacher led us to a big, black, iron box with round holes in the top. The box was so hot that I could feel the heat even from three feet away. "Is this thing a stove?" I whispered to the student next to me.

The girl stared. "Haven't you seen a stove before?"

I shook my head. She laughed. She laughed even harder when it came time to beat a bowl of eggs. I wanted to show that I was willing to work hard. I beat the eggs so vigorously that most of them spilled on the floor.

One day we had to cut little red radishes in the shape of flowers. "What's the point?" I asked. "Once you put a radish in your mouth and start chewing, all your hard work will be wasted!"

"The art of radish sculpting is important," insisted the teacher. "The radish flowers add a touch of graciousness to your dinner table."

Personally, I believed that only some real Chinese food would add graciousness to my landlady's dinner table, but I obediently did what the teacher told me. I wanted to master the use of a kitchen knife. The only time I had held a knife before, I had been digging out a bullet. Through sheer determination, I did manage to improve, and my fellow students congratulated me when I finally fashioned a radish into something resembling a rose.

I was so elated that I had to write about my success to Ailin that very evening. So far I had had nothing to write about except how difficult school was for me. I wanted to tell Ailin about my successes, not my failures. The home economics course finally gave me some progress to report.

Dear Ailin,

Yes, I'm very eager to go to San Francisco and try your cooking. But you may even be able to sample MY cooking someday! I'm taking a course called home economics, and it's supposed to make me better at cooking, sewing, and other skills necessary for an American housewife. Don't laugh! I'm learning to sculpt a radish into a rose. Do you do that in your restaurant?

You never tell me how hard you have to work in your restaurant, only that the business is improving. But now that I've done some kitchen work myself, I'm beginning to have an idea of what you go through every day.

Yanyan

If cooking was hard for me, sewing was even worse. The first time I handed the teacher the grubby handkerchief I was hemming, she looked at it incredulously. "I thought Chinese girls are supposed to be experts at sewing! Their embroidery is exquisite, simply exquisite!" It took a while to convince her that not all Chinese were capable of exquisite embroidery, and that I had trouble even threading a needle.

In my English class, I had hoped to improve my pronunciation. Instead, the class concentrated on studying great works of English literature. We started out with *Beowulf,* which had been written more than a thousand years ago. When I looked at the first page of the book, I thought I had picked up a German book by mistake. It even sounded like a foreign language when the teacher started reading a passage, and it certainly didn't help with my pronunciation of English. The language of *Beowulf* is as different from modern English as Classical Chinese is from modern spoken Chinese. Well, I had learned some Classical Chinese in our family school back home. If I could manage that, I thought grimly, I could learn *Beowulf* too.

I was dismayed to find out that even my best subject, mathematics, was hard for me. I was one of only three girls in the mathematics class, and I discovered that the other two girls were very, very good. Soon the three of us began sitting together, to give one another support.

A couple of the boys in the class made a point of jeering at us whenever we made mistakes. The first time I gave a wrong answer and heard a boy snicker, I thought it was because of my Chinese accent. Then I heard even louder snickers and snorting noises when one of the other girls made a mistake.

"They don't like us here," one of the girls said to me. Her name was Maureen, and she had short, red curls, which she pulled nervously when she was thinking hard. We had a little time to chat before we went to our next classes.

"Why don't the boys in the mathematics class like you?" I asked. "You're just as good as they are—better, sometimes."

"That just makes them madder," Maureen said bitterly. "They think science and mathematics are men's subjects, and that we're invaders."

It reminded me of what my advisor had said about sciences not being suited to the female mentality.

"Girls should take home economics classes," said the other girl, Ellen, putting on a high, mincing voice. "Young ladies should learn the womanly arts, so that they will become fitting wives and mothers."

I laughed. She reminded me of something too: Second Brother used to lecture me about how I had to behave modestly, so that I would make a fitting wife and mother. "So girls in this country have to keep their places, too," I said. Then I thought of something. "But at least you American women don't have to suffer the torture of having bound feet."

The two girls were interested in what it was like to be a woman in China. "Is it also true that you're not supposed to understand things like mathematics?" asked Maureen.

I thought about my mother and my female cousins. "Actually, Chinese women are supposed to be good at figures. They have to keep track of the family money, for instance."

"Women keep track of money?" exclaimed Ellen. "So their position is not so low, after all!"

"A woman's position *is* low," I said. "That's why she handles the money. It's supposed to be too unimportant for a scholar and a gentleman to think about."

Both Ellen and Maureen were astounded. "Money is supposed to be unimportant?" cried Maureen. "Wait till I tell my father that!"

"Sometimes I wish I had gone to a women's college," Ellen said, after the boys in the mathematics class had been particularly nasty one day and the teacher had done little to stop them. "Then I wouldn't have to listen to all these jeers!"

"I'm not sorry I came to Cornell!" declared Maureen. "It takes guts to study so-called men's subjects. I'm determined to prove that I can do it!"

Guts? I was puzzled at first by her reference to intestines. I finally guessed that she meant the equivalent of what we Chinese call *qi*, in other words, courage.

Maureen and Ellen were the first friends I made at Cornell, and I felt a little less lonely than before. But I didn't see much of them after classes, because they were staying at a dormitory. I had to tramp downhill back to Mrs. Harte's house every day.

I didn't have a chance to make any friends in my other classes, either. In my physics class, I thought I saw a Chinese boy among the students. The class was big, and he was sitting on the other side of the room. When the bell rang, everyone rushed out. I hugged the wall, to stand out of the way of students running for their next class. By the time I looked around for the Chinese boy, he had already gone. I thought he looked a bit like one of the two boys I had seen in the Chinese restaurant.

The physics course involved a weekly session in the laboratory, but compared to cooking and sewing, the lab experiments were relatively easy. I was the only girl in my lab session. Whenever I made a mistake, the teaching assistant would give a loud sigh of impatience. He always answered curtly when I asked him a question.

I thought at first he was annoyed because my female mentality was unsuited to lab work. Then I discovered another reason. One beautiful fall day, many of the students were eating their lunches on a patio with a gorgeous view of Cayuga Lake. Carrying my tray, I went outside and looked for a place. The physics teaching assistant was sitting at a table with a friend. His back was toward me, but I could recognize his disagreeable, nasal voice anywhere.

"That Chinese girl is not only clumsy, she doesn't have the proper mental discipline for a subject like physics," he was saying.

I felt the heat rushing into my face as I realized that he was talking about *me*.

"Yeah, you're right," said his companion. "Those Orientals have brains that are fundamentally different from ours. Even the shape of their skull is different! The Chinese do all right as long as they stick to light, wispy things like that Taoism of theirs. But you can't expect them to cope with a hard science like physics, which requires a logical mind."

Angry tears blurred my eyes as I turned and made my way back into the cafeteria. I felt like giving that teaching assistant a good kick in the intestines. Then a scene in a railway car suddenly popped into my memory: Eldest Brother and Baoshu were discussing how the shape of a foreigner's nose made it impossible for him to master Chinese, and how his deep-set eyes prevented him from seeing subtlety in art—all this they said in Mr. Pettigrew's hearing.

So the physics teaching assistant was only ignorant, not deliberately malicious. Very well, then, if he thought I suffered the double handicap of being both a female and a Chinese, I would use all my guts to pass that physics course, just to show him how wrong he was!

During those grueling early days at Cornell, I worked so hard that I didn't have time to be homesick. Every night I fell into bed exhausted by hard work and exercise, and went to sleep without even dreaming. Or if I had dreams, I forgot about them during my frantic morning rush to gulp down breakfast and struggle up the hill to school.

Even on weekends, when there were no classes, I had to work from morning to evening, just to keep from falling behind in my work. I saw very little of the downtown part of Ithaca. I did go there once to pick up my laundry. As I stood waiting for my turn, a man came inside, and when he saw me he said, "You put too much starch in my shirt! It's as stiff as a board!"

Totally baffled, I just stared at him. "Just try to do a better job next time!" he snapped when I didn't reply.

I finally realized that he was mistaking me for an employee at the laundry. "I don't work here," I told him. "I'm a student at the university."

He was the one who stared this time. "Well, I'll be doggoned! I did hear there were Chinks at the university. Never thought I'd see one in person, though."

He used several words I didn't recognize, so I said nothing. I took my bundle of laundry, and as I climbed back to Mrs. Harte's house, I thought over what the man had said. I couldn't make any sense of the dog that was gone, but from the context, I suspected that *Chink* was his term for a Chinese. It didn't sound very nice, the way he had said it. Maybe he expected all Chinese to work in a laundry, not study at the university. On the other hand, *I* had thought that all Indians wore feathers in their hair and lived in tents.

Again, I was reminded that people got annoyed when things didn't come out as they expected. A Chinese husband called his wife *neiren,* "person of the inner chamber," because she was supposed to stay shut away and out of sight. Men became furious when their wives came out and spoke their minds. Foreigners too expected all Chinese women to be meek and downtrodden. I remembered that Miss Scott had become furious with me when I spoke up in class and told her that there had been powerful women in Chinese history, such as the late Empress Dowager of the Qing dynasty.

In spite of unpleasant encounters like the one in the laundry, my life wasn't totally bleak. On Sundays, I went to dinner with the Pettigrews. It was like going home—a little bit.

"Just look at this poor girl!" Mrs. Pettigrew exclaimed on one of my visits. "Why, she's down to skin and bones! I'll have to feed her well and build her up again!"

The two Pettigrew boys, who were fourteen and fifteen years old, treated me like a younger sister because they were much taller than I was. Also, there was so much I didn't know that they had to teach me.

American sports was a subject the boys were most eager to talk about. At Cornell sports were important, because it was believed that they promoted "manliness" in the male students, the same way that home economics promoted "womanliness" in female students.

The boys were avid fans of a game called football, and they did their best to explain the game to me. They weren't very successful. First of all, I couldn't understand why it was called football, since the players hardly used their feet at all.

One Saturday, the Pettigrews invited me to go with them to a football game between Cornell and Yale. I was astounded by the loud yells of the spectators. It sounded like a revolution breaking out, except that what I had seen of the revolution in China had not been quite so noisy.

Nor could I make any sense of the game, since all I could see was a big muddle, with the players crashing into one another. Having possession of the ball was apparently very important, but I never did catch a glimpse of it. At least I could tell which players were on our side and which were against us: The Cornell boys wore red, and the Yale boys wore blue.

Suddenly there was a huge roar, and all the spectators around me jumped to their feet. From the yells, I gathered that someone had downed a touch—or maybe touched a down. Whatever it was, it was obviously a good thing.

After the roaring died down, somebody blew a whistle, and the players left the field. A file of musicians playing various instruments marched across the field, reminding me of an old-fashioned Chinese funeral.

"It's halftime," said Mr. Pettigrew. When I didn't understand, he explained. "It's like an intermission. Boy, I can use a rest from all this excitement."

Not having been excited, I didn't need a rest, but I was glad to get up and stretch a bit, since I was stiff from sitting on a hard bench for so long. As I stood up, I heard voices speaking Mandarin Chinese behind me. I whipped around and saw three Chinese students—the same three I had seen before.

One of the boys met my eyes. "Are you Chinese?" he asked. "I remember seeing you in the Peach Garden restaurant."

I couldn't help it. I broke into a big smile. "Yes. I'm from Nanjing, and this is my first time in America."

He also smiled. "I think you're in my physics class, too."

So he *was* the one I had seen! I didn't realize that he had noticed *me* as well. "My name is Zhang Xueyan," I told him.

"Mine is Gao Lihong," he said. "But please call me L.H. We all use the initials of our given names, because it's convenient and it sounds informal."

His friends had overheard our exchange, and they both turned to look at me. "Hey, it looks like we've got a new addition to our group!" said the other boy. "I'm Y.C."

I remembered how long I had addressed Baoshu by his full name, Liang Baoshu, because it would have been unacceptable socially to use only his first name. I rather liked this use of initials. It was informal and gave a sense of togetherness without specifically breaking Chinese etiquette.

The third Chinese student, the girl, said shortly, "I'm Celia."

So. It would seem that while boys used their initials, girls used their English names. That was also a compromise, since using an English first name felt somehow less shocking than using a Chinese first name. What bothered me was that it made the status of male students different from that of female students. Also, I disliked my English name, Sheila, which I used only with Americans. I didn't *feel* like a Sheila.

But it couldn't be helped. "I'm Sheila Zhang," I muttered.

The boy called L.H. smiled and said, "Hello, Sheila, I hope we see more of you."

Before he could say anything else, Celia pulled at his arm. "We'd better go back to our seats. The third quarter is about to begin."

I was so happy at having met the three Chinese students that I hardly noticed what was happening on the football field during the second half of the game. Our side must have won, because when we got up to leave at the end, people were beaming and saying things like, "Great game, wasn't it?"

Down on the field, a number of spectators were running around, yelling and tooting little horns that squawked and bleated. The eyes of the Pettigrew boys were shining, and their parents had a hard time preventing them from joining the noisemakers. Even Mr. Pettigrew, who didn't usually display his feelings, discussed some of the more thrilling moments of the game with a friend, and praised the skills of the star quarterfront—or was it quarterback?

"I can tell you had a wonderful time, too, Sheila," said Mrs. Pettigrew.

I nodded. "Yes, I did. This was one of the best days I've had since I came to Ithaca."

* * *

Dear Ailin,

Today the Pettigrews invited me to watch a sport called football. It was very confusing, and I had no idea what was going on. All I knew was that each team wanted to get the ball past the other team to something called the end zone. Have you had a chance to see a football game? I know how busy you are. But I hope you have a chance to take a little time off.

I met three Chinese students today who are also attending Cornell. I hope to get better acquainted with them.

Yanyan

Dear Yanyan,

No, I haven't attended a football game, although some of our customers talk about the game, since it seems to be important in America. I do have more free time than before. Our restaurant is doing well enough so that we can afford to hire someone to help with the dishes and the cleaning. When I'm free, I like to walk in the park or along the beach.

I'm glad you managed to meet some fellow Chinese

students. Our restaurant is in the Chinatown area, so we
see lots of Chinese people. You'll find it very interesting
here if you come and visit.

Ailin

* * *

I had thought that time would creep by very slowly and that my four years at Cornell would last an eternity. But time went by surprisingly fast, and before I knew it, the days were getting shorter and the leaves started changing color.

In Nanjing, we made trips to the countryside every autumn to enjoy the beautiful red leaves. But the leaves in Nanjing were nothing compared to the ones in Ithaca. Whole streets of trees changed to a scarlet color so brilliant that they seemed to be on fire. I also loved the way the piles of fallen leaves crunched under my feet when I walked through them.

I could keep up with Sibyl's strides now, and in my classes, too, I was keeping up somewhat better. The big surprise was in my English class, where I got one of the best grades on a midterm test. Maybe it was because I had studied harder than any of the others. Also, the rest of the students found the old language of *Beowulf* as strange as I did.

In fact, I had almost as much trouble with modern English as with the Old English of *Beowulf*. Individual words I could always look up in my dictionary, but the words were often combined into phrases that turned out to mean something quite unexpected. One day I heard Mrs. Harte mutter, "I really have to pull myself together and get my housework done sooner."

I puzzled over the phrase *pull myself together*. I looked at Mrs. Harte, and she didn't seem to be coming apart in any way, or even to be loose. Why did she have to pull herself together? Finally I took Sibyl aside and asked her to explain. When she stopped giggling, she told me that Mrs. Harte simply meant she had to stop wasting time and make a stronger effort. I thanked her and decided that I rather liked *pulling myself together*. It gave the impression of being solid, hard, and determined.

In my home economics class, I finally succeeded in beating the eggs for a cake batter without spilling a single drop. Unfortunately, I forgot to put in baking powder, and my cake came out flat and leathery. It was tougher than the soles of my cloth shoes in China.

I made progress in my physics class too. Even the teaching assistant was unable to find fault with my lab work. I didn't manage to talk to the Chinese boy, L.H., but we were now sitting only a few rows away instead of being across the room from each other. There were more than a hundred students in the class, which was held in a large lecture room, but most of the seats were taken by the time I arrived, so I had little choice. I always got there fairly late from my home economics class, which was some distance away on campus. Maybe L.H. had a long way to walk too.

I was beginning to lose hope of meeting the Chinese students again. Since I lived down the hill, I wasn't on campus much after classes. Where those students lived, I had no idea.

As schoolwork became slightly easier for me, I began to have a little free time on weekends. One Saturday, Sibyl asked me if I would like to get some exercise by taking a walk with her near Cascadilla Gorge, where the maple trees were particularly brilliant.

A month earlier, I would have laughed at the very idea of going out for more exercise—except that I wouldn't have had any breath left for laughter. But now I agreed eagerly to Sibyl's suggestion. For once I had done most of my homework, and I could afford a relatively leisurely weekend.

The air had a nip, a taste of what winter might bring. I didn't mind. Back home, the sharp autumn air was something we welcomed, because it meant an end to the notorious Nanjing summer heat. Sibyl and I shuffled happily through the crisp leaves.

At the edge of Cascadilla Gorge, I peered down and was impressed by how deep it was. A fall into the gorge would mean certain death. We continued our walk, and before we had gone far, I heard voices—Chinese voices.

Rounding a bend, I saw the three Chinese students I had met before, and with them was another woman student, also Chinese. "There's Sheila!" cried the student called L.H. "We wondered when we'd see you again!"

I was warmed by the smiles of the Chinese students—except for the look on Celia's face. It was more of a pout. I introduced Sibyl to them, but it was clear that they had no interest in her, an American woman, and an older one at that.

In fact, the fourth student, also a woman, looked older than the rest as well. "I'm Loretta Feng," she said. "I'm majoring in biology."

Finally, I had an opportunity to talk to my fellow countrymen without having to rush off somewhere. "Do you all live in dormitories?" I asked.

"Loretta and I live in a dorm," said Celia. She didn't look happy about it. "The boys don't live on the campus."

"Y.C. and I have rooms nearer downtown," said L.H. "It's cheaper than living in a dormitory."

"I rent a room, too!" I cried. I indicated Sibyl. "We're staying at a house on Seneca Street owned by a Mrs. Harte, and it's about halfway up from downtown."

"Mrs. Harte's house on Seneca Street," said Y.C. "I think I know where it is."

"Do you walk here often?" L.H. asked me. "I come here a lot because I like the view here at the gorge. It reminds me of a Chinese landscape painting."

"We haven't got all afternoon!" said Celia before I had a chance to answer. "Come on, we'd better go if we want to do any canoeing."

L.H. waved good-bye to me and followed the others, who started walking briskly down the hill. Sibyl watched them go with a smile. "I didn't understand a word of the Chinese, but I could tell that boy was interested in you, Sheila."

"I don't know what you're talking about," I said in confusion.

"You'll find out," said Sibyl. "I can also tell that girl called Celia is pretty miffed about it."

How could Sibyl really understand the feelings of people speaking a different language? Perhaps what she had detected in L.H. was simply his satisfaction at finding another Chinese student at Cornell.

What about my own feelings? After refusing to run away with Baoshu, I had made my decision to pursue a medical career. I wasn't interested in another boy.

CHAPTER 8

The very next Monday afternoon, just after I returned home from the university, Mrs. Harte knocked on my door. "There are a couple of boys here looking for you," she said.

I thought they might be the Pettigrew boys with some message from their parents. Instead, I found L.H. and Y.C. standing on Mrs. Harte's front porch. They looked very pleased with themselves. "So we did find your rooming house!" said L.H. "I looked up all the people in Ithaca called Harte, and I found one with an address on Seneca Street."

"We're wondering if you'd want to come to our place for some Chinese food," said Y.C. "Celia and Loretta are cooking."

I didn't think that the two girls had issued the invitation. But I could tell from the sulfurous smell that Mrs. Harte was boiling cabbage again for dinner. Her usual way of cooking vegetables was to boil them in a big pot of water until they turned grayish yellow. Chinese food, cooked by anybody, sounded heavenly. I immediately agreed to go with them.

Sibyl was in the dining room when I told Mrs. Harte that I wouldn't be home for dinner. She gave me a meaningful smile, which I pretended not to notice.

The boys were staying at a house in a part of town close to the canal that fed into Cayuga Lake. Although I knew almost nothing about American houses, I could tell that the homes in this area were less well-to-do than those in Mrs. Harte's neighborhood. The houses here were set closer together, and some of them had peeling paint.

L.H. told me that the landlady was willing to let them use the kitchen occasionally for preparing Chinese food, after the rest of the roomers had finished their dinner. "She's glad to let us do it. On days when we don't eat her food, she has two fewer mouths to feed."

When we arrived, Y.C. told me that Celia and Loretta were in the kitchen. He seemed to take it for granted that I would join the girls. I found the two girls chopping vegetables.

"Hello," Loretta said to me. "I see that Y.C. has enlisted you as a cook."

Celia looked at me without enthusiasm. "What can you do?"

I couldn't think of anything. "I can make radish roses," I finally offered.

To my relief, my offer was declined. "Why don't you join the boys?" suggested Loretta. "Since this is your first time, you can be our guest."

In the dining room, the boys were setting the table. I offered to help, although the only thing left for me to do was to set out the chopsticks. I picked up a pair and caressed them. They were plain and made of bamboo, not like the ivory ones we had at home, but it felt wonderful to have a pair of chopsticks in my hands at last, after weeks of eating with knives and forks.

"We didn't mean to put you to work right away," L.H. said apologetically. "We just wanted a chance to get acquainted with a new arrival from China. Are you a freshman?"

"I'm not a regular student yet," I admitted. "I applied too late, but I was allowed to enter as a special student. If I do well in my courses this semester, I'll be able to enroll as a freshman. What about you?"

"Celia and I are sophomores, Y.C. is a junior, and Loretta is a graduate student," said L.H. "We're Boxer Scholarship students. What about you?"

I knew about the Boxer Scholarships. The Boxers were a group of Chinese fanatics who believed that they were invulnerable to bullets and other Western weapons. In 1900, they attacked the foreign legations in Beijing and inflicted many casualties before foreign troops entered the city and put down the rebellion. In reparation for the attack, the Chinese government was forced to pay enormous sums of money to the foreign governments involved. A number of them, including the United States, decided to use part of the reparation money to finance scholarships for Chinese students attending universities in those countries. Every year, competitive examinations were given to choose recipients for these scholarships.

I looked at the two boys with respect. They had to be very smart to win Boxer Scholarships. "I'm not a Boxer Scholarship student," I admitted. "My father is paying for my education."

Celia entered the dining room, carrying a dish of stir-fried meat strips. "Your father is paying for everything?" she said. "Your family must be really rich! I hope you won't despise this poor food we're serving here."

"No, no, of course not!" I said hurriedly. "It smells wonderful! I hope I can learn to cook like this someday!"

I was perfectly sincere. The meal prepared by the

two girls, consisting of three dishes and a soup, truly tasted like a banquet to me. I said as much, and Loretta smiled her thanks at my compliments. Celia just looked sour.

"It's very kind of Loretta and Celia to feed us like this," said L.H. "I have a weak stomach, and I'm not sure I could have survived months of eating nothing but heavy American food."

It was true that L.H. did not look very robust. Not much above average in height for a Chinese, he looked taller because he was very thin. There was a hint of a stoop in his posture. If he had worn a mandarin's gown and hat, he could have easily passed for the hero of a Chinese opera, the one who always had to be rescued from the villain by a woman warrior. I began to see why Celia seemed protective, maybe even possessive, of L.H. Was that why she resented me as a potential competitor?

She didn't have to be afraid of competition from me. She was pretty, while I never claimed to have remarkable looks. Furthermore, my relationship with Baoshu had left me wounded and unwilling to enter into another one.

Y.C., the other boy, was more solidly built than L.H. and did not seem to have any digestive problems. He ate heartily, so heartily that Loretta snatched the omelet dish out of his reach. "Hey, the rest of us have to have some too, you know!" she said, and she was only half joking.

We all ate well, even L.H. We didn't leave a single scrap of food at the end of the meal. Back home this would have been bad manners. Mother had taught me that we were supposed to leave a portion of every dish for the servants, even the best dish—especially the best dish.

But there were no servants here. If I wanted to be accepted by the others and continue eating Chinese meals like this one, *I* had better learn to do what our servants did: I had to wash vegetables and slice meat, stir-fry them together, and boil rice. I would even have to wash dishes and scour pots. I had a sudden vision of my friend Ailin doing all of that.

As we ate, I learned a few things about the others. L.H.'s father had been a tutor for a wealthy family in Wuxi, a beautiful city not too far from Nanjing. His father had given L.H. a thorough grounding in the Chinese classics and had intended that his son become a scholar like himself. But L.H. had seen Halley's comet appear in 1910, when he was seven years old. He had never forgotten that remarkable sight, and when he later learned more about comets, he developed a strong interest in astronomy. That was his major at Cornell.

"I still remember the first time I peered through a

telescope here and saw the rings of Saturn!" he said. I could hear the passion in his voice. He had found a subject he really loved.

Loretta's family was originally from Canton, but they had moved to Shanghai after the revolution in 1911. Her father, like mine, had traveled in Europe and spoke several languages. "I've no idea where I picked up my interest in biology," she said. "Maybe it was after my father returned home from Switzerland with a sprig of edelweiss."

"Did any of your professors tell you that a science like biology is not a proper study for the female mentality?" I asked.

Loretta laughed. "How did you know?"

"That's what my advisor told me," I said. "But I took a physics course anyway. It's turning out to be really hard, and I'm almost sorry I took it."

L.H. looked alarmed. "Are you thinking of dropping it and taking something easier?"

"No, I hate to admit defeat," I said. "I'm going to stick with it no matter what."

Y.C. wanted to be an engineer. (I wondered if his advisor had told him that the shape of his skull was wrong for studying engineering.) Y.C. wanted to work on building railroads, which was also his father's career. The railroads in China had been built largely with the help of the British, although Germans and Belgians were responsible for certain stretches. But Y.C.'s father wanted him to study American railroads. After all, America was a huge country, like China, and there had to be efficient ways here of constructing railroads for long-distance travel.

Celia was from Sichuan, famous for its peppery food. Maybe that was where she got her peppery temper. In spite of her remarks about my wealthy family, Celia's own family was far from poor, I discovered. Her father was an antiques dealer. Both Loretta and Celia had learned to cook in Ithaca. Like me, neither one had had any experience at all before coming to America.

I went back to my rooming house feeling more hopeful than I had since arriving in Ithaca. The food left me full but not stupefied, the way I usually felt after one of Mrs. Harte's heavy meals of meat and potatoes. The best treat of all was finding companionship at last.

A week later, I was invited again. Since I couldn't contribute to the cooking, I brought along a big bag of apples, which were very good in Ithaca. They were crisp and sweet, better than any I had eaten in Nanjing.

But even the apples couldn't make up for the fact that I was a guest—a guest not invited by the two girls who had done the cooking. Celia was openly disgruntled at seeing me, while Loretta was merely tolerant.

During dinner Celia began to talk about her major,

which was English literature. "I'm going to be a writer," she announced. "I want to join all those writers who are turning away from Classical Chinese and adopting the language of the common people instead. This is the most important development in the history of Chinese literature!"

I had heard about this movement to write in the vernacular, that is, the language used in daily life. Until the twentieth century, serious literature in China had all been written in Classical Chinese, which required years of study to understand. After the revolution, there was a movement to write in everyday language understood by the common people. Father was an enthusiastic supporter of this movement and told us that great English writers, such as Dickens, wanted everyone to understand their works. But Eldest Brother and Second Brother thought the movement would debase literature. They felt that all serious writing had to be done in Classical Chinese, understood only by the elite few.

"You're right: Good writing should be accessible to all the people," I said to Celia. "I've always loved popular novels written in the vernacular, such as *Dream of the Red Chamber* and *Journey to the West*. They're easy to understand, and they're really enjoyable."

Celia looked deeply offended. "I'm not talking about

popular novels! I intend to write *serious* literature, not something intended to be enjoyable or easily understood!"

"I thought you said you wanted everyone to understand," I protested.

"*You're* the one who doesn't understand!" snapped Celia. "Our movement uses the language of the common people, but that doesn't mean we expect all the common people to understand our work!"

"Then why not stick to Classical Chinese, if you don't want to be understood?" I asked. I wasn't being sarcastic. I really wanted to know.

Celia gave a huge sigh. "I give up! It's hopeless trying to explain things to you!"

I gave up too. It was hopeless trying to win Celia's goodwill. "Well, then you must really love *Beowulf*," I said. "That's pretty hard to understand, although it turned out to be more enjoyable than I expected. I love the fight scenes with the monster."

"Fight scenes!" cried Celia. "Is that all you care about? I suppose you'll tell me next that you enjoy martial arts!"

The mention of martial arts brought up an image of Baoshu, and I felt a terrible ache in my chest. I shut my eyes against tears that threatened to well up.

"Celia, you mustn't be so hard on Sheila," L.H. said gently. "Not everyone shares your taste in literature."

Far from soothing Celia's feelings, L.H.'s comment made her even angrier. I left soon afterward. I didn't expect to be invited again in the near future. And I wasn't.

• • •

The weather became much colder, and the nights longer. In her last letter, Ailin had mentioned the wonderful warm weather in San Francisco.

Dear Yanyan,

It must be getting colder in Ithaca. Here in San Francisco, it's as warm as September in Nanjing. How about visiting us? I'd love to see you again.

Ailin

Dear Ailin,

I want to see you, too. But I don't see how I can find time to cross all the way to the West Coast. I have so much schoolwork to do that I haven't even visited places such as Taughannock Falls, Watkins Glen, and other nearby scenic spots.

Maybe at a later time, we can get together.

Yanyan

The cold weather made me think of Baoshu. As I looked at the bare tree branches outside Mrs. Harte's house, I pictured myself galloping with him across the Manchurian plains. At times like these, I tormented myself with thoughts of "What if . . . What if. . . ."

Eating Sunday dinner with the Pettigrew family helped ease my loneliness and isolation. The two teenaged boys treated me like a member of the family. They enjoyed teasing me when my English became too bizarre.

Mr. Pettigrew asked me about my schoolwork. "I really have to struggle in my physics course," I told him, "but if I pull my guts together, I think I can pass it."

Hearing *pull my guts together,* the two boys burst out laughing so hard that they almost fell off their chairs.

One Sunday dinner at the Pettigrews was less pleasant, however. That night they had some other guests, a Mr. and Mrs. Winthrop, also faculty members at Cornell. Before going into the dining room, the guests sat in the living room and drank something called sherry, which was a bit like a rice wine. I passed around a dish of nuts. The boys usually did that, but they were at a friend's house that evening.

Mrs. Winthrop spilled a little of her drink on the low table in front of her. She turned to me. "Get me a cloth to wipe it up," she ordered.

I was a little startled by Mrs. Winthrop's curt tone. Was that her normal way of speaking?

A little later, I found out the reason for her manner toward me. When Mrs. Pettigrew came out of the kitchen and started to chat with the guests, Mrs. Winthrop said, "I'm so glad you finally broke down and decided to hire yourself some help, Mabel." She glanced at me and added, "Chinese girls can work very hard, but is her English adequate? Can she understand you well enough to follow orders?"

"I can muster up enough English to follow orders and mop up your spilled drink," I snapped before I could stop myself.

Both Mr. and Mrs. Pettigrew turned crimson, and Mrs. Winthrop's jaw dropped almost to the floor. "It's my fault, Gloria," Mr. Pettigrew said to Mrs. Winthrop. "I should have introduced you. Sheila isn't our maid. She's a student at Cornell, and we like to invite her over for Sunday dinners."

The dinner was not a great success. I fought down a temptation to show off my command of English by quoting *Beowulf.* I didn't think it would be appreciated.

By the time I returned to Mrs. Harte's and prepared for bed that night, I was finally cool enough to think about Mrs. Winthrop's mistake without anger—at least without red-hot fury. She was no worse than the man in the laundry who thought all Chinks worked at laundering.

Besides, I had no right to be offended because Mrs. Winthrop had mistaken me for a maid. Back home in China, we employed maids ourselves. Furthermore, Ailin had had to work as a nanny and was now working as a cook and probably a waitress, too. Ailin might look delicate, but even without any training in the martial arts, she was strong. Since I prided myself on my courage, I had to ignore slights from people like Mrs. Winthrop and the physics teaching assistant. I had to pull my guts together and be as strong as Ailin.

※　※　※

Autumn passed all too quickly. One night rain mixed with sleet fell, and by the next morning the streets were coated with ice. Climbing up to the university was like struggling up a glass mountain, but going back down was the really treacherous part. Just as I thought I had made it safely back to Mrs. Harte's house, my foot slipped and I landed heavily on my bottom.

"Let me help you up," said a voice. I had been concentrating so hard on keeping my footing, I hadn't noticed that L.H. had been walking behind me. He reached down to offer his hand but then slipped himself and landed right next to me. We looked at each other and burst out laughing.

Although I hadn't been eating dinner with the

Chinese students, I did see L.H. regularly in my physics class. We had gradually worked our way closer to each other, and by now we were sitting only one row apart. It was possible that some of the other students had noticed us and were deliberately making things easier.

We finally struggled back to our feet, and by carefully sliding and skidding, managed to make it to my front door. I turned to say good-bye to L.H. and noticed a couple of yellowish bruises on his cheek. "You've had a fall already," I said.

He looked away. "Well, not exactly."

He didn't say anything else and seemed uncomfortable about the subject, so I didn't press him. They were old bruises, I decided, since they had already turned yellow.

After that, I often found L.H. walking back with me from the university. Sometimes we didn't go directly back to Mrs. Harte's house but took a longer route by way of Cascadilla Gorge. It was one of L.H.'s favorite places in Ithaca, and he always paused there to admire the scenery before moving on.

We talked about the physics course, which I still found fiendishly hard. "I'm beginning to be really sorry I took the course," I said. "I've discovered that it involves using calculus, which I'm just beginning to study in my math course."

"Why did you take it, then?" he asked curiously. "Most students take the course in their second year, after they've had a year of freshman math."

Why did I take it? It was a good question. I decided to answer honestly. "The advisor was ordering me to do this and do that—take home economics, English, and so on—so I decided to take something totally unexpected."

He said nothing. I began to feel a little foolish. "I know it was a silly reason for choosing a course. That just proves how childish I was!"

Then I saw that he was grinning. "But I like your reason for taking the course: doing something totally unexpected!"

So far, I'd found that people became annoyed, even angry, when you did something unexpected. They wanted you to conform to their idea of what you should be. Chinese were expected to be experts at laundry, girls were expected to do exquisite embroidery, and Westerners with big noses were not expected to be able to speak Chinese. People liked you to be predictable because it made them feel safer.

It was very refreshing to find that L.H. actually approved of someone doing the unexpected. Not only did he enjoy the unexpected, he was fascinated by the unknown, by the distant stars. He was adventurous—not physically, but mentally. I had never met anyone like him before. If I weren't careful, I might grow to like this boy—like him too much. Suddenly I wondered if Baoshu liked people who did the unexpected.

Once, when L.H. and I were walking together, I noticed that he looked more sallow than usual. He gave a little burp and winced. "Sorry, a touch of indigestion."

I remembered something Eldest Brother had learned from his martial arts teacher and had passed on to me: Avoid any kind of strenuous exercise after eating heavily. "Did you eat a particularly heavy lunch today?" I asked L.H.

He grimaced. "How did you guess? It was one of my landlady's thick stews."

"Well, you should always avoid exercise after a heavy meal like that," I told him. "And I consider climbing up to the campus heavy exercise."

"Yes, doctor," he said meekly, and smiled. But he began to look thoughtful.

A couple of weeks later, I noticed that L.H. was looking less gaunt than before. "Has your digestion improved?" I asked. "You seem to have better color, and you've gained weight."

"Yes, Doctor Zhang, I'm eating better," he said with a grin. "I took your advice about not eating too much before strenuous exercise, and it seems to work!"

I was absurdly pleased. Of course I enjoyed being addressed as Doctor Zhang, even though he had said it as a joke. What I enjoyed even more was that my advice had really helped his digestion. When I had first decided to become a doctor, I was intrigued by the various ways you could treat people. I was fascinated by germs and how they affected the healing of wounds. Now it gave me a wonderful feeling to know that by studying medicine, I could really help people become healthier. It made me more determined than ever to become a doctor.

As the days grew shorter, it would be dark by the time I started walking back from the university. I wanted to be independent, but I felt safer on the days when L.H. walked back with me. I wondered if Celia knew about the time we were spending together.

One evening, L.H. walked with me as far as Mrs. Harte's house, and when I had gone up the steps to the front porch, I heard voices behind me. I turned around and saw that L.H. was talking to a group of three boys. They were all very big, almost twice his size.

"It won't take you more than a couple of minutes!" one of them said. He sounded angry.

"I can't do it," said L.H. "It's dishonest."

"Dirty Chink!" said another boy. "Let's give him a lesson he won't forget!"

I heard the sound of a blow. L.H. was bent over, holding his head.

Suddenly I found myself rushing down the steps.

Eldest Brother's words came back to me: "A half turn, lean forward, and kick back at the same time."

I kicked. It was a good kick, and even with Chinese cloth shoes it would have connected painfully. Delivered with my heavy leather shoes, the impact sent the boy whooping and gasping for air.

The other two boys stood frozen in surprise. Not only was my attack unexpected, I was so much shorter than they were that they didn't see me until it was too late.

I aimed another kick at a second boy, but it didn't land quite so satisfactorily. Nevertheless it also connected.

"Now you're three against two, instead of three against one!" I shouted at them. "How do you like that, you bullies?"

I had a loud voice, as my mother kept telling me. My shouts brought Mrs. Harte out to the front porch, where she was joined by Sibyl. The three boys, still somewhat dazed, looked around and decided to take off.

I went over to L.H., who had a new bruise on his face in addition to the older, yellow ones. "I suppose those boys were the ones who caused your other bruises?" I asked.

He nodded. Then he looked at me in wonder. "You're a martial arts expert!"

"No, I'm not," I muttered. "I'm just a beginner. At the moment I feel more like a singer in a second-rate Chinese opera. I'll break out into a falsetto aria next."

Sibyl came down the steps. "Come on, Sheila, let's get this boy inside and put some ice on that cheek."

The use of ice to reduce swelling was new to me, and I resolved to find out why that worked. Mrs. Harte's icebox contained a huge hunk of ice, delivered once a day to keep the food cold. Sibyl chipped a piece off, wrapped it in a towel, and gave it to L.H., who held it against his cheek.

As Mrs. Harte busied herself preparing dinner, L.H. and I sat at the dining table and I asked him quietly about the attacks. "Those boys wanted you to do something, and you refused."

He grimaced. "They're football players, and they're taking an elementary mathematics course. They found it too hard for them, so they wanted me to do their homework for them."

"How did they happen to choose you, particularly?" I asked.

"One of my classmates is a keen football fan," he replied. "When he heard about the problems these boys were having, he thought I could help, since math is one of my best subjects."

"You mean giving them some tutoring?"

"If it were just tutoring, I would be glad to help. But the boys didn't want to do any of the work at all! They claimed it interfered with their football practice. They wanted me to write all their homework papers for them. When I refused, they started threatening me."

"I still don't see why they picked *you*. There are lots of people at the university who could have helped them."

He sighed. "You must have noticed that bullies prefer to pick on the weak, and I look like someone easy to push around. Besides, since I'm Chinese, people won't rush to help me when they see me attacked." He grinned at me—a painful grin because of his swollen cheek. "Of course they didn't expect a woman warrior from a Chinese opera to come to the rescue."

"They also didn't expect you to refuse," I said. "What will they do now? Do you think they'll attack you again?"

"I doubt it," he said. "But if they do, I'll just have to keep on refusing."

He might look like a weakling, the effeminate scholarly type seen in so many Chinese novels. But he was unexpectedly tough inside. Like Ailin, L.H. didn't have to practice martial arts to be brave.

◆ ◆ ◆

To my surprise, I found myself enjoying the home economics class more and more. I was actually learning to cook! Well, not to cook, exactly, but to prepare vegetables for cooking. The teacher demonstrated a vegetable shredder one day, and I was amazed at how quickly it sliced the cabbage. So many Chinese dishes involved slicing things finely that this machine seemed to be the solution to preparing Chinese food.

That was when I decided to buy a shredder and give a dinner party. At the time, I thought it would be a courageous thing to do. Later, I realized that I must have been insane.

Since I hadn't been invited back to eat with L.H., Y.C., and the two girls, I thought my best move would be to invite *them* to Mrs. Harte's house for dinner. Following their example, I would cook a Chinese dinner after the rest of the roomers at Mrs. Harte's boardinghouse had finished eating.

When I saw L.H. again and told him about the invitation, he raised his eyebrows and looked at me. I noticed that the latest batch of bruises had faded to yellow, and there were no fresh ones. "Are you sure you want to do this?" he asked.

That was not the enthusiastic response I had hoped to get, but I nodded. "Yes, I am," I said firmly.

It was hard to cook Chinese food without soy sauce, ginger, tofu, and other Chinese ingredients. I was reluctant to ask Celia and Loretta where they had bought their supplies. Then I thought of the Peach Garden restaurant. I had gone back there once, and on my second visit the cook had prepared a meal closer to what I used to eat at home. I could ask the owners of the restaurant where they bought their supplies.

It turned out that the owners ordered their supplies from New York City. They bought soy sauce by the gallons and rice in 100-pound sacks, and had it all shipped up to Ithaca.

Very well, then. I would have to prepare a Chinese dinner without those ingredients. Instead, I would stir-fry the dishes—that is, cook them quickly over a hot fire. That should make the food taste more Chinese.

I bought a vegetable shredder and three heads of cabbage, returned to Mrs. Harte's kitchen, and went to work. Thirty sweaty minutes later, I had a mound of shredded cabbage—actually, a mountain of shredded cabbage. To stir-fry this, I would need a cooking pan the size of a laundry tub.

I heard a snort and saw Sibyl standing by the kitchen door, trying to stifle her laughter. "What are you going to do with all this cabbage?" she asked when she could speak again.

"I was going to stir-fry it—you know, cook it the Chinese way," I said. "Maybe I can do it in small batches."

"You'll still be doing it at midnight," said Sibyl. "What else are we going to have?" I had also invited her to my novice dinner, but now she didn't seem to look forward to the treat.

What else were we going to have? That was when I realized that I hadn't done a thing about the other parts of the dinner. I had bought a whole chicken, still undressed, a piece of pork, still unsliced, and some rice, still unwashed.

I sat down on a kitchen chair and put my head in my hands. I had some hard thinking to do. It dawned on me that preparing a dinner was not a matter of doing one dish at a time. It was true that at home, our chef took only minutes to cook each dish, and the maids brought them to the dining table one at a time. But the *preparation* for all the dishes must have been done a long time in advance. In fact, I recalled that my home economics teacher had said something along these lines. I should have listened to her more carefully.

What should I do? My guests would be arriving in about an hour, and all I had was a mound of shredded cabbage. Rice, which took the longest to cook, should have been the first to be prepared. The only rice I had been able to find in Ithaca was something used by Americans for rice pudding. What kind did the Peach Garden people serve?

The Peach Garden! I leaped up from my chair. "Sibyl, I need your help to carry some food back!"

The owner of the Peach Garden restaurant was willing to prepare a few dishes of Chinese food for me to take away. Having his customers eat the food at home was new to him. But after thinking it over, he smiled and agreed. In fact, he liked the idea, since it kept the tables in the restaurant free for other diners.

Sibyl and I waited nervously while the cook busied himself in the kitchen, but in the end we were able to carry off three hot dishes and a pot of rice. Hauling the food up the hill without spilling was tricky, but we managed to make it back to Mrs. Harte's house with minutes to spare before the guests arrived. I even had time to set the table—with chopsticks I had wheedled from the Peach Garden restaurant.

The look of amazement on the faces of L.H., Y.C., Celia, and Loretta was comical. I didn't know what they had expected, but it certainly wasn't a complete Chinese dinner. Y.C., always the hungriest, was the first to sit down and help himself to some stir-fried prawns. The others followed more slowly, but it didn't take long for them to start eating almost as heartily.

"The Peach Garden restaurant, right?" asked Y.C. when he paused for breath. "I thought I recognized the orange-colored sauce."

I couldn't hide the truth from them. "Yes, this food

all came from the restaurant. I tried to make the cook cut down on the sugar for the sweet-and-sour pork, but I couldn't do anything about the orange color."

"Naturally we can't expect our wealthy young lady here to soil her hands by doing any actual cooking," said Celia. "It's only paupers like ourselves that have to do our own work."

"I really started to prepare the meal myself," I said. "I even shredded a huge mound of cabbage. But I soon found out that cooking is much harder than I expected."

"Of course it's hard!" snapped Celia. "You don't think we learned to do it instantly, do you?"

"Now I finally appreciate all the work you did," I said humbly. "And I want to thank you for having invited me to eat with you."

"That's nice of you to say so, Sheila," said Loretta, who seemed touched.

"I think we ought to thank Sheila for inviting us to this delicious dinner," said L.H. "Whether she cooked it herself is irrelevant. It's the kind thought that counts."

"I agree!" said Y.C.

I thought that on the whole the dinner was going pretty well. Then Celia asked about the ruckus in front of Mrs. Harte's house. "I heard that you attacked some football players," she said. "With your taste in literature, I should have known that you were a martial arts expert!"

"I'm just a beginner," I said. "My brother gave me some lessons."

"Yes, but to throw yourself at those boys, that took real belligerence!" said Celia.

"Well, L.H. was being beaten up, and I had to do something," I retorted. "What would you have done if you had been there?"

That stopped her. For the rest of the meal, Celia was pretty much silent. My guests—the majority of them, anyway—ate well and thanked me warmly when they left. Maybe I would be accepted as a member of the group, after all.

CHAPTER 9

Winter arrived, and I began to understand why Father had warned me about the cold. I had often felt cold in Nanjing, especially in the mornings when I jumped out of bed and landed on the icy floor. But I had not been prepared for the bitter cold in Ithaca that burned my face and made my eyes ache when I trudged up the hill in the mornings.

All around me in class I heard people discussing what they intended to do during the winter vacation. My classmates seemed totally preoccupied with the holiday of Christmas.

I remembered that back in Nanjing, the teachers at the MacIntosh School used to put up wreaths and pictures of the Christ child in a manger, surrounded by sheep, cows, and other farm animals. We sang songs associated with the holiday, called carols. But in my family, Christmas meant little more than an exotic Western festival.

Here in Ithaca, the streets were full of Christmas decorations. Mrs. Harte bought a cut tree, and with help from the two male tenants set it up on a stand in the living room. It was so tall that it almost touched the ceiling. I loved the fragrance of the fresh green branches. Sibyl and I helped Mrs. Harte hang tiny glass figures on the branches of the tree. I was very, very careful with them. They looked so fragile that I was sure if I dropped one on the floor, it would shatter into little pieces.

Everyone I knew seemed to be going away during the three weeks of the winter vacation. Ellen and Maureen were going home to Cleveland and Buffalo, respectively. "I can't do any real work at home," complained Maureen. "I've got two brothers, and their idea of a good time is to provoke me into yelling at them."

Her mention of her brothers made me think of mine. Suddenly I longed to hear Eldest Brother's gruff voice, telling me that I was making progress in kung fu. I even wanted to hear Second Brother's voice, scolding me and telling me that I was an insufferable brat.

I asked Sibyl what she intended to do during the

winter break. "I'm going home to my folks in Elmira," she said. She had left home five years earlier to lead an independent life, but she always went home during the Christmas holidays. It was a time when families got together.

I thought I had gotten over my loneliness, but now it all came rushing back. At least the Chinese students wouldn't be going back home. It would take too long and cost too much. They should still be around during the vacation.

L.H. looked uncomfortable when I asked him about his plans. "There's some talk about New York City," he finally confessed. But he didn't mention details.

Two days later I learned more. I was finally invited back to the boys' rooming house for another dinner. During the meal, Celia brought up the subject of New York City. "I have a cousin there, and he has invited us to stay with him for the holidays." She looked around. "He's including L.H., Y.C., and Loretta, of course."

The others didn't meet my eyes. Celia continued. "Too bad my cousin doesn't have room for another person. But I'm sure Sheila has plans to go somewhere else. She can afford to travel much farther than New York City."

I found it difficult to swallow another bite. The food

suddenly seemed greasy and unappetizing. Before I realized it, I found myself saying, "As a matter of fact, I *am* planning to travel during the winter vacation. I've decided to visit my friend in San Francisco."

Two days earlier, I had received another letter from Ailin. Her days were still filled with arduous labor, but things were improving for her and her husband.

Dear Yanyan,

Business is so much better that James has finally decided I can take one day off each week. It's wonderful to have a whole day in which I can do anything I want!

How I wish you could come and visit us! I'd love to show you around San Francisco and let you see how beautiful the city is.

What about coming during the Christmas holidays? Don't you have a few weeks off from school?

Ailin

It didn't occur to me that I might actually take Ailin at her word and go visit her. I had far too much homework to do, and San Francisco was at the very opposite end of America. I still remembered the long train ride I had taken with the Pettigrews to cross the country.

At the dinner party with the other Chinese students, I had declared my intention of going to California because I wanted to show them that I had my own resources, and I wouldn't be pining all by myself while the rest of them went to New York City.

I decided to consult Mr. and Mrs. Pettigrew about the trip. They had invited me to spend Christmas Day with them, but I knew that Mrs. Pettigrew's sister and family would be staying with them, and she would have her hands full with her houseguests.

When she heard about my plans, Mrs. Pettigrew was horrified. "Why, you poor girl, you'd have to spend four nights by yourself on the train! And that's just one way!"

"I don't mind traveling alone, Mrs. Pettigrew," I said. In fact if I stayed in Ithaca, I would be spending most of the vacation alone, anyway.

Mr. Pettigrew looked at me thoughtfully. "I think Sheila can do it. She's one tough young lady," he added with a small smile.

It seemed news of my encounter with the football players had leaked out. The Pettigrews must have learned about it from Mrs. Harte, and their sons were soon asking me to give them all the details. The boys were entranced, but they were very disappointed when I told them I didn't have time to give them lessons in kung fu.

Finally, after many warnings about not speaking to strangers, the Pettigrews arranged my trip to the West

Coast. They even accompanied me on the local train as far as the junction with the transcontinental train bound for San Francisco.

* * *

Compared to the trip from the West Coast I took with the Pettigrews, this trip seemed both longer and shorter. This was winter, and the green farmland we had passed before now looked bleak and bare. Without the Pettigrews telling me about points of interest along the way, the hours and days seemed long and monotonous. The route to San Francisco was more southerly than the one from Seattle, and there were stretches of nothing but desert.

In another sense, though, time passed more quickly for me. The long train ride gave me a chance to do a lot of homework and study for the final exams that would take place a month after the vacation ended. I was reading the Middle English of Chaucer when the train passed through Kansas, and I was practicing taking derivatives in Colorado. There were very few distractions, and I didn't even have to make the stiff climb up to the university from Mrs. Harte's house. In fact, I missed the exercise.

Once we left Nevada and entered California, I became too excited at the prospect of seeing Ailin again, and I gave up trying to study. The train trip ended at the station in Oakland, a city on the east side of San Francisco Bay.

I had written to Ailin, telling her about my time of arrival. But since my train was almost an hour late, I wasn't sure if she would be able to meet me. When I got down to the platform with my suitcase, I looked around but didn't see her. By the time most of the other passengers had left, I still saw no one that looked like Ailin. My heart fell. What could I do? I didn't think I would be able to call a rickshaw to take me to her restaurant in San Francisco.

Then I saw that there was a young lady looking anxiously around, as if meeting a passenger. I blinked and looked again. It couldn't be, but it was! It was Tao Ailin!

At that moment she looked in my direction and shook her head in disbelief. "Is that really you, Yanyan?"

We rushed together and hugged, laughing and crying at the same time. It was a while before we could say anything that made sense.

"You look like a grown-up!" I managed to gasp. "I would never have recognized you!"

"You've lost so much weight!" she said. "I can't believe that this is the old Zhang Xueyan who loved dumplings so much!"

It had been a year and a half since I saw Ailin off at

the docks in Shanghai, but now it seemed like only yesterday. We reverted to our schoolgirl talk as we chatted and made our way to the ferry that would take us across to the city. There was so much to say to each other that I hardly noticed the view of San Francisco and the bay.

Ailin told me about some of the dishes she was trying to cook in the restaurant. She made light of her failures, but I suspected there was a lot she wasn't telling me. I described my mishaps in the home economics course. "Hey, maybe you should get a cabbage-shredding machine!" I said. When I told Ailin about the huge mound of cabbage I had produced, she laughed so hard some of the other passengers turned to look at us. Until this moment, I had not realized how lonely I had been all these months.

When the ferry approached the docks, we became more serious. I looked at my old friend and saw her work-worn hands. "Are you sorry you decided to stay in America and run a restaurant?" I asked.

"Life has been hard, but I'm not sorry," she replied quietly. I could see that she was telling the truth. Suddenly her face brightened, and she started waving. "There's James! He took time off to meet us, after all!"

There was so much joy in her voice that my throat tightened with emotion.

As we took the cable car from the ferry dock to

Chinatown, I peered at the man Ailin had married. In one of her letters, she had told me that James was almost ten years older than she was. He was pleasant looking, but not outstandingly handsome. For an instant I thought of Baoshu and his striking looks.

During the noisy, lurching cable car ride, I didn't get a chance to exchange more than a few words with James, but in his eyes I saw humor and gentleness as he looked at Ailin. She had chosen well.

"Here we are," said James when we arrived at our stop. He took my suitcase and helped me climb down.

We walked a short distance up a street and entered the door of the restaurant that Ailin and her husband owned. It was called *Peng Lai,* after a mythical isle in Chinese folklore. In spite of its poetic name, the restaurant was a small place, not any bigger than the Peach Garden in Ithaca. Inside, it was crowded with customers. A harassed-looking man rushed up to James and started talking excitedly. I realized that they were speaking Cantonese, which I didn't understand.

Ailin took me to the back of the house and we mounted the stairs to the second floor. "I'm afraid I'll have to go back down and help out," she said. "The restaurant is very busy because it's Friday."

She showed me to a small room overlooking an alley in the back. "This is our only spare room. You'll have to push aside those boxes so you can put your suitcase down."

"My room in Ithaca is no bigger," I said quickly. "Don't worry about me."

Giving me a quick smile, Ailin turned and hurried downstairs. I felt guilty, inviting myself to stay when they had their hands so full already. But Ailin had looked so happy to see me that I wasn't sorry I had come. I lay down on the bed for a short rest, and the next thing I knew, I opened my eyes to find that it was dark. I looked at my small travel clock and saw that it was eight-thirty in the evening. I heard someone coming up the stairs, and Ailin poked her head in. "Oh, good. You're awake. We have time to eat some supper now. Let's go down."

The staircase still smelled of cooking—Chinese cooking—and I found myself ravenously hungry. In the dining room there were only a few customers left. Most of the customers were Chinese, and they ate early. Ailin led me to one of the empty tables. "You'll be eating my cooking tonight. Are you willing to take a chance on it?"

"After months of corned beef and cabbage, what do you think?" I said.

While Ailin went to fetch food for us, James was with the last of the customers, putting their leftover food into small paper cartons.

"Do your customers usually take food home with them?" I asked when the customers were all gone and James sat down with us to eat.

"Yes," James admitted. "All the Chinese restaurants here provide paper cartons for taking home leftovers. The customers always order more than they can finish, and it would be a great waste to throw all that food away."

It was true that we Chinese expected to have some food left over at the end of the meal. Having the platters completely empty was shameful, because it implied that we were too stingy to prepare any extra food. If there were leftovers, the servants ate them. But here in America, where not many families had servants, the customers themselves ate the leftovers.

I thought of the time I bought food from the Peach Garden in Ithaca, and I had an idea. "Why don't you prepare food that's especially meant to be taken away and eaten at people's homes?" I said eagerly. "You can use your paper cartons for that."

James stared at me. "That's not a bad idea! Is this something you learned at the university?"

I looked down. "No, I was stupid enough to invite some Chinese students at Cornell to a dinner party that I was hoping to prepare myself—" I stopped when

Ailin started to giggle. I glared at her. "Well, you didn't become a great cook overnight!"

Ailin stopped giggling. "No, it took weeks and weeks of practice. I was cooking for the Warner family, and they were very patient with me." She grinned. "But then they didn't have much choice. It was either my cooking or Mrs. Warner's wooden pork chops."

I didn't know what wooden pork chops were, but they couldn't be as bad as corned beef and sulfurous cabbage.

James turned to Ailin and smiled. He had an attractive smile, which immediately made him handsomer. "Your friend has a good head for business!"

"How can you say that?" protested Ailin. "Yanyan plans to be a doctor!"

"We don't always end up doing what we intended, do we?" I said gently. Ailin herself had had plans to be a teacher, but she had to give them up when her uncle took her out of school. My remark wasn't meant to be cruel. Seeing Ailin's contentment as she smiled back at James convinced me that she had not been hurt.

During the next few days, I tried to help Ailin in the kitchen. By the third day, I was actually doing more good than harm. I was assigned the job of washing and slicing vegetables, and my skill with the knife improved. Just being in the kitchen with Ailin gave me a warm feeling of camaraderie.

Finally Ailin had enough confidence in me to let me approach the stove itself. I was allowed to stir some of the food while it cooked over the blazing fire belching out of the open hole of the stove. Wielding the black iron spatula, I felt almost as powerful as if I held a sword in my hand. Was that why my parents always spoke to our chef with so much respect?

Being allowed to do some of the actual cooking gave me confidence, and I begged Ailin to teach me at least one dish that I could master all by myself. "Why?" she asked, laughing. "Are you planning to open a boarding-house for Chinese students?"

"You're right about the Chinese students part," I said. "I want to invite those students again and show them that I don't have to buy all the food from the local Chinese restaurant."

We settled on a recipe for sour-hot soup. "It's a Sichuan dish," said Ailin. "When we tried it on our customers, it became a great hit and people come in asking for it especially."

I liked the idea of the sour-hot soup. Celia was from Sichuan, and it would give me great satisfaction to serve her something from her home province.

With instructions from Ailin, I learned to thicken

the soup stock with some starch, then add vinegar and black pepper to make it taste sour and hot. "You can add chopped vegetables, bits of meat, or beaten eggs—anything you want. It's a good way of using up leftovers," she added.

"I can beat eggs," I said. "But I'm not sure I want to put in any of Mrs. Harte's leftover corned beef or cabbage."

Ailin finally had her day off, and we took the cable car to a part of San Francisco that I hadn't seen before. We walked along a windswept bluff that faced the ocean. Since coming to America, I hadn't been near the sea, and seeing the foamy waves reminded me that a wide ocean separated us from our home in China.

"Are you planning to live in America for the rest of your life?" I asked.

"Yes," Ailin replied without hesitation. "This is now my home, and this is where I plan to raise a family someday." After a moment she turned to look at me. "What about you? Are you returning to China?"

"Yes," I said, also without hesitation. "I'm glad I'm attending Cornell University. They have a good medical program, and I want to complete my medical training. But there is nothing in this country that holds me here."

Ailin looked at me curiously. "You sound very lonely. Haven't you made any real friends at all in America?"

I immediately thought of L.H., but he was in New York with Celia and the others. I thought of Maureen and Ellen, the two girls in my mathematics class. I liked them, but I had no opportunity to spend much time with them. I thought of Sibyl and the Pettigrews. They were good to me, but they were much older. "No, you're my only true friend in America, Ailin."

"What about that dinner party you're planning to give?" asked Ailin. "Isn't that for some friends?"

"They are some Chinese students at the university that I was hoping to know better. But they aren't particularly eager to be friends with me." Then I realized that I was doing an injustice to L.H. "Well, there is one boy who is nicer to me than the rest."

"Really?" asked Ailin, immediately looking interested. "What is he like?"

I discovered that I actually felt shy about discussing L.H. "Well, he's thin, and he suffers from indigestion," I said weakly, and stopped.

Ailin laughed. "I can tell that he must have made quite an impression on you. Do you like him?"

"I don't have a chance to like or dislike him," I muttered. "He's guarded by a dragon called Celia, who breathes fire whenever she sees me near him."

We walked along the sandy path for a while, past tufts of coarse grass. Ailin broke the silence. "You said once that you didn't intend to get married, and that you planned to support yourself. Do you still feel that way?"

I thought of Baoshu, and as always I felt a sharp pang. "There is someone I nearly married . . ."

Ailin stared at me. "You never said anything about this in your letters!"

The barrier broke. I found words pouring out at last, words that I hadn't dared to say to anyone, not even Ailin. I told her about Baoshu, about our train trip to Shanghai, and about our growing attraction to each other. Ailin's eyes grew wide when I described Baoshu's escape from the police, his gunshot wound, and my primitive surgery in digging out the bullet.

"He asked me to run away with him," I said at the end. My throat felt tight, and I had trouble getting the words out. "I would have had to give up everything, all my plans and my medical studies!"

Ailin looked gravely at me. "Are your medical studies really so important to you?"

"At first I was interested in medicine only because of curiosity," I admitted. "I wanted to know why some treatments worked, and why some didn't. Then I realized that I loved even more the thought of being able to make people well." I stole a look at her and went on. "There are some diseases that cause so much suffering that we simply have to find a cure. Tuberculosis, for instance."

Ailin closed her eyes. Her father, whom she loved deeply, had died of tuberculosis. But I had to go on. "I knew that curing people was important to me, and that I had to continue my studies."

"You didn't want to give up your studies and help Baoshu fight for his beliefs?" asked Ailin. She had put her finger on the most sensitive part of my relationship with Baoshu.

"I think I would have made the sacrifice if I had thought he had deeply cherished beliefs," I said slowly. "But the truth is that Baoshu loved danger for its own sake, and he wanted me to go with him because he thought I shared that love."

"He was fighting for the restoration of the Manchu dynasty, you said," Ailin said. "Since he's half Manchu, I can understand that he would want that."

"That's what I thought at first," I said. "But he's also half Chinese. You can't just throw that half away."

"Maybe he believed that China was in turmoil and needed an emperor to restore law and order," suggested Ailin.

"That's what he said to my father," I said. "But I'm not sure how much he believed it himself. I think it was the excitement that he craved."

I remembered how James had looked at Ailin with love and pride. Without her help, the restaurant could not have succeeded. She was a full partner.

It was different with Baoshu. I finally came to what had caused me to reject him. "Baoshu wanted me, but what he wanted was a follower and a companion to share his adventures."

Ailin looked at me long and hard. I saw both pity and admiration in her eyes. "Yes, I think you did the right thing in refusing Baoshu."

CHAPTER 10

The trip back to Ithaca didn't seem nearly as long as the trip to San Francisco. When I wasn't studying, I stared out the window at the passing scenery, and I treasured the memory of Ailin's face as she waved good-bye to me at the train station. She looked assured and proud. She had every right to be.

After the warmth and sunshine in California, the stinging cold in Ithaca hit me like a blow. My teeth were chattering as I walked out of the train station, but by the time I trudged up the hill to Mrs. Harte's house, I was warm from the exercise. The climb was worse than usual because of the ice and slush underfoot.

Mrs. Harte and Sibyl welcomed me back with genuine affection, and that warmed me even further. "Too bad you missed a good snowstorm last week," said Sibyl. "But don't worry, we'll have plenty more before the end of the season."

On the first day of my physics class after the winter vacation, I found myself sitting next to L.H. "It took a whole semester," he said, grinning. "But we finally managed to get adjacent seats."

I looked down, suddenly a little shy. It was an unusual sensation for me. "So how was your trip to New York City?" I asked, changing the subject.

"A huge, busy city like that was exciting, after being in this isolated town for so long," he replied. He started to say something, but the professor came in just then, and we had to turn our attention to the lecture.

At the end of the class, instead of rushing away, L.H. walked along with me. "I don't have to go to my philosophy class, because we're doing independent study and writing papers for the rest of the semester," he explained.

We made our way carefully across the campus, trying to avoid the patches of hard, packed snow. "How was your trip to the West Coast?" L.H. asked.

"I spent the whole time in San Francisco doing kitchen work in my friend's restaurant," I said. I glanced at him to see how he took the news.

He skidded and fell flat on his back. I laughed as I helped him to his feet. "I even learned to cook . . .

well, just a little. I brought back all sorts of good things from San Francisco: dried scallops and shrimp, pickled mustard greens, and soybean paste."

As L.H. still stared, I continued, "One of these days, I'm going to invite all of you for a dinner I'll try to cook myself. In fact, my friend gave me a recipe for Sichuan sour-hot soup, which should please Celia."

L.H. finally found his voice. "You always like to do the unexpected, don't you?"

He had said this before, meaning it as a compliment. I accepted it as such. We were arriving at my home economics class, and I could hardly wait to show the other students how much I had improved in cutting up vegetables.

Just as Sibyl had predicted, we began to get snow-storms, one after another, throughout January. The streets were lined on either side with walls of accumulated snow almost as tall as I was. It was tough work just to get up the hill to the university. Giving a dinner party was out of the question.

I hardly noticed the snow, since I became totally immersed in studying for the final examinations, which started a month after the winter vacation. The examinations were vitally important to me. Their results would determine whether I could enter the university as a regular student next semester.

In spite of my fears about the examinations, I relished the challenge. At the MacIntosh School, most of the subjects had been easy for me, and I seldom found the examinations taxing. Here, I faced examinations so hard that I had a drowning sensation while taking them. The Cornell school song began with "Far above Cayuga's waters, with its waves of blue. . . ." It was all I could do to keep my head above those waves of blue. Nevertheless, I found the struggle exhilarating.

After taking my last exam, a period of anxious waiting began. I didn't want to talk to people, even sympathetic ones such as Sibyl, and I spent most of the time sitting in my room, writing letters.

Dear Ailin,

I don't know if I passed my examinations or not, but I enjoyed the fight. What I enjoyed even more was telling people that I spent the winter vacation working in your kitchen and learning to cook. At the earliest opportunity, I'm going to try out your recipe for the sour-hot soup!

The visit with you not only brought me the comfort I needed, but also cleared up some things in my mind. Thank you, dearest friend. I hope we can see each other again soon.

Yanyan

When our grades were finally out, I was tremendously relieved to learn that I had passed all my courses. As expected, my lowest grade was in the physics course, where I barely squeaked by. L.H. consoled me. "You should have taken the course in your sophomore year. Most students do."

"I know," I admitted. "My advisor kept telling me it was too hard for me, and I took it just to show him he was wrong and to prove how brave I was. Now I know it wasn't courage, just recklessness."

"So will you drop the physics course during the second semester?" asked L.H.

"No, I'll try to stick with it," I said. "I made a mistake, and I'm prepared to pay for it. I hate to give up."

I didn't do too badly in the mathematics course, although my score was far behind those of Maureen and Ellen. To the disgust of many of the boys in the class (and probably of the teacher as well), the two girls received the top grades.

In English, I managed not to disgrace the language of Shakespeare completely, but the biggest surprise came in my home economics course, where the teacher wrote that I was the student showing the greatest improvement, and deserved a special mention for striving so hard.

For the second semester, therefore, I could enroll as

a regular freshman instead of a special student. Passing my exams also meant that I would be living in a girls' dormitory on campus, instead of in a rooming house. Boys could live in rooming houses in the town, but regular girl students were required to live in university dormitories. The advantage was that I wouldn't have to go up the hill twice a day, a grueling climb during the winter. But I also felt sad at the thought of leaving Mrs. Harte and Sibyl. They were the closest thing I had to a family in Ithaca.

Another advantage to living in a dormitory was that I'd have a chance to see more of the other students, such as Maureen and Ellen. Even Celia would have to accept me as a regular student.

• • •

There was a short break between the end of the examination period and the start of the new semester. It was too short for people to travel out of town, but long enough to unwind after examinations.

On Sunday, I was invited as usual for dinner at the Pettigrews'. I arrived shortly after noon at their house, looking forward to the warmth of the family and a boisterous welcome from the two boys.

When the front door opened, Mrs. Pettigrew stood before me with a broad grin on her face. "We have a big surprise for you, Sheila!"

In the living room, I found Mr. Pettigrew talking to a stranger. Then I took another look and received a stunning shock. It wasn't a stranger. It was Baoshu.

When I had seen him last, he had been an exhausted, ragged rickshaw man with a straw hat over his head. The only thing I managed to say was, "Are the police still after you?"

Baoshu laughed. Recovering from my shock, I took a good look at him. His hair was neatly cut, and he was wearing a Western suit. He looked quite at home in it.

Mrs. Pettigrew looked puzzled. "My dear," Mr. Pettigrew said to his wife, "the last time I saw this young man was on a train, and he was being rather rude to a Big Nose sharing his compartment. Now it seems that he's a suave diplomat, representing the Manchu government in exile."

"Is this true?" I asked Baoshu. "This isn't just another one of your disguises?"

He smiled. "It's my real identity, believe it or not. I'm actually working for the Manchu government, now in residence in Japan. Since my father was an imperial official before the revolution and my mother is Manchu, it was natural for them to appoint me."

Mrs. Pettigrew became impatient with the exchange, which was in Chinese. "Let's go in to dinner. The food will be getting cold."

We sat down at the table, joined by the two Pettigrew boys. For a while the conversation was about winter sports in Ithaca. Baoshu's English was heavily accented, but he spoke it well enough to ask the boys about skiing, something he had never tried. They went on to talk about ice skating on Beebe Lake, and Baoshu described his own skating experiences on the lake in Beijing's Beihai Park.

After dessert the boys went off to see some friends, and Mrs. Pettigrew went to the kitchen to clean up. As usual I offered to help, and as usual she refused. "I've got a lot more practice now," I reassured her. "After helping out at my friend's restaurant, I've learned to wash dishes without breaking or chipping them."

"No, my dear, I don't need your help," she said. Then she winked. "Go talk to your friend. I had no idea you were hiding such a glamorous beau!"

I joined Mr. Pettigrew and Baoshu in the living room, where they were discussing the possibility of bringing back the emperor. "Do you really think you have a chance?" Mr. Pettigrew asked. "I have the feeling that the time is past for an imperial restoration. In addition to the warlords, there are various groups with growing support, such as the Kuomintang, the Communists, and others."

"You may be right," admitted Baoshu. He did not

look discouraged, however. "What I hear discussed among the exiles is the possibility of forming an independent country of Manchuria."

"If the Manchus form an independent country, so will the Mongols, the Tibetans, various Muslim peoples, and all the other minorities!" I cried indignantly. "China will be broken up into pieces, just as it was during the Warring States Period. There would be endless fighting, and our country would bleed to death!"

"That's exactly what's happening in the Balkans," said Mr. Pettigrew. He looked sharply at Baoshu. "You don't seem displeased at the prospect of endless fighting."

"But we have endless fighting right now," Baoshu pointed out. "It's time for stability again."

I studied him. There was a glitter in his eyes, a hunger for excitement. Stability might be boring for someone like him. Mr. Pettigrew thought so, too. "You know, young man, I don't believe you're cut out to be a diplomat. At heart you're really an adventurer!"

Baoshu laughed. "You're probably right," he said, apparently taking Mr. Pettigrew's remark as a compliment.

"Why did you really come to this country?" I asked him. "Did you think you'd find support here for the idea of an independent Manchuria?"

He nodded. "You'd be surprised how many Americans would like that. We're also finding that the Japanese are strongly in favor of an independent Manchuria ruled by PuYi, the last Qing dynasty emperor."

"Many people prefer to see China weak and divided," murmured Mr. Pettigrew. "A strong and united China would seem too threatening."

"Is that what you want, Baoshu?" I demanded. "To see China weak and divided? Or do you consider yourself a Manchu and not Chinese at all?"

Mrs. Pettigrew entered the living room, carrying a tray with cups of coffee. "My, my, such serious faces!" She turned to her husband. "George, I'm sure you're boring our guests with all your political talk."

She distributed the coffee and passed the cream and sugar around. Our conversation switched to English, and Mrs. Pettigrew asked Baoshu what other places in America he had visited.

"New York City and Washington, D.C., chiefly," he replied. "And of course I had to visit Ithaca, knowing that Miss Zhang is attending school here. I remembered that Professor Pettigrew was from Cornell, and that's why I found my way to your house."

"How did you know I was attending school here?" I asked.

He smiled. "Oh, I have my sources."

"I'm sure where there's a will, there's a way," Mrs. Pettigrew said archly.

After finishing his dessert and coffee, Baoshu thanked his hostess and rose to take his leave. "It was very kind of you to invite me," he said to Mr. Pettigrew. He grinned and added, "Especially after I was so rude to you on the train."

He turned to me. "It's a nice sunny day for a walk. We have some things to talk over, Yanyan."

He was right. There were still things that had to be said.

Outside, I automatically led the way down the path toward Cascadilla Gorge. In the bright sunlight, the snowy mounds on either side of the path dazzled the eyes. Baoshu strode along as if he enjoyed the squeaky feel of crunching down on the snow. He was a northerner, and reveled in the cold and ice.

We stopped just before we reached the edge of the gorge. "You've lost a lot of weight," Baoshu said, examining me.

"You mean I'm no longer a juicy morsel?" I said before I could stop myself.

He smiled. "You're still the same old Yanyan, after all. I'm glad."

We were in danger of falling into our old relationship, the one we had in that Shanghai alley. I pulled myself together. "No, Baoshu, I'm not the same old Yanyan. I'm grown up now."

He was still smiling. "I hope this doesn't mean you've lost your taste for taking risks."

"No, but I'm not taking risks for the sake of taking risks," I said. "I'll do it only for something I believe in."

Baoshu's face also became serious. "I want you to leave Ithaca and come with me, Yanyan."

"I've already told you that I can't," I said. "There is no place for me in your world."

"But there is! There will be an imperial court again, and as my wife you will have rank and honor."

I shook my head. "Can you really see me as one of the court ladies? I can't sit still, and my voice is too loud. I would die of boredom within a week."

"Then come with me for the sake of adventure!" he said. His eyes were bright. "I promise that you won't be bored. We'll have many dangers and obstacles to face. Doesn't that tempt you?"

Again I shook my head. "Not even the prospect of digging out more bullets. Don't you see, Baoshu, adventures are for children. I'm an adult now, and I want to become a doctor. Here at Cornell I have a chance to get the training I need."

"Need? But *I* need you, Yanyan! Come with me!"

"No, I can't," I whispered.

Baoshu took a step closer.

"She has already said she can't," said L.H., stepping

forth. He had been standing out of sight around the bend. Wearing a thick winter coat, he still looked like a stooped, undernourished scholar from a Chinese opera.

"Go away," said Baoshu, sparing L.H. only a brief, contemptuous glance.

"Only if you leave Sheila alone," said L.H.

Baoshu started to laugh. "Who is Sheila?" He turned to look at me and laughed again. "Do you really answer to the ridiculous name of Sheila?"

I began to feel angry. I hated the name Sheila, but that was for me to decide. I resented having Baoshu decide for me what was ridiculous and what was not. "The name Sheila is good enough for my *friends*," I said between my teeth.

"We've wasted enough time," Baoshu said impatiently, and reached out for me. "Let's go, Yanyan."

"I won't let you take her," said L.H.

Baoshu turned slowly, and for the first time he took a good look at L.H. "Are you proposing to stop me?"

Huddled inside his coat, L.H. looked cold. "Yes."

I suddenly realized that we were standing at the edge of the gorge. Baoshu realized the same thing. "You know," he drawled, "if you get in my way, I can easily toss you into the gorge."

"No, you can't," said L.H.

"Why not?" asked Baoshu. He sounded genuinely curious.

L.H. pointed to me. "Because if you do, she will despise you for the rest of her life."

Baoshu stared. For the first time, he appeared uncertain as he looked from L.H. and back to me. A chunk of ice fell from a tree branch and dropped into the gorge. I heard the sound of it hitting bottom, a long way down.

"Come with me, Yanyan," Baoshu said once more.

"No," I said for the last time.

Baoshu seemed to swell with rage. As he stepped forward, L.H. placed himself in front of me, barring the way.

The two of them were standing so close that they shared the foggy white breath between their faces.

I truly believe that if L.H. had used the word *hate* instead of *despise,* then Baoshu might have carried out his threat. But L.H. had understood Baoshu's character, and he knew that contempt was the one thing Baoshu could not tolerate.

Something inside Baoshu seemed to collapse. The bright anger on his face dimmed. Slowly he turned and started to walk away, but after two steps, he stopped and looked back at me. "I'm not giving up, Yanyan," he said. I couldn't tell whether I heard hope or despair in his voice.

Baoshu's crunching steps died away. That sound would haunt me for a long, long time. Suddenly, my legs gave away under me and I sank down on the snow. I found that I was weeping. "I never knew that growing up could be so painful," I sobbed.

After a while I heard L.H.'s voice. "What I like about you is that you always do the unexpected."

I tried to wipe my cheeks, but the mixture of tears and mucus made a messy smear. "What didn't you expect? That I would grow up?"

"No, I didn't expect you to cry," he replied. "I knew that you had already grown up."

I tried to struggle to my feet, and L.H. reached down to give me a hand. "When d-did I g-grow up?" I asked. My throat was scraped raw from crying, and it hurt to talk.

"When you admitted that you had been too rash to take that physics course but declared that you would keep on with it next semester." He smiled. "It takes courage to grow up."

"It took courage for you to step in front of Baoshu," I said. "He was not making an idle threat about tossing you into the gorge."

"I knew it was not an idle threat," L.H. said. "But some things are worth the risk."

I began to shiver uncontrollably. L.H. unbuttoned

his coat and wrapped it around both of us. I had to lean on him for support, because my legs were still weak.

But the support wouldn't always be one-sided. I had saved L.H. from the bully football players, and in the future he might accept my help again. Baoshu, on the other hand, would always insist on being the strong one.

The image of Baoshu had lodged in my chest like a bullet. L.H. had helped with its extraction, and the operation had been excruciating. But now that the bullet was out, the healing could begin.

The warmth I shared with L.H. finally stopped my shivering, and we began to climb back together from the edge of the gorge.

A Note on the
Manchus, Manchuria, and Manchukuo

The Manchus are a non-Chinese people from the northeastern region of China called Manchuria, which now occupies the provinces of Liaoning, Jilin, and Heilongjiang. The Manchu language is related to Mongolian and others of the Turkic family.

In the middle of the seventeenth century, the Ming dynasty of China had become corrupt and incompetent, and the country was torn by rebellions. The Manchus, aided by some Chinese rebels disgusted by the Ming regime, seized the opportunity to launch an invasion of China.

The conquest of China by the Manchus was successful, and in 1644 they occupied Beijing and set up a new dynasty called Qing. The Manchus compelled all

Chinese men to adopt the Manchu hairstyle of a shaved forehead with a long pigtail in the back. Manchu women did not bind their feet, and the new rulers tried, unsuccessfully, to make Chinese women abandon this ancient practice.

The early Qing emperors, notably Kangxi and Qianlong, were vigorous and able. During their reigns, China enjoyed a long period of prosperity and stability. But as with other dynasties, the later emperors became indolent and decadent. Power fell into the hands of eunuchs, dowager empresses, and scheming courtiers.

During the nineteenth and early twentieth centuries, China suffered a series of humiliating defeats at the hands of foreign powers, most notably during the Opium Wars, the Taiping Rebellion, and the Boxer Rebellion. Britain, America, France, Germany, Russia, and Japan tried to carve up China, as they had done with Africa and much of southeast Asia.

In 1911, the Manchu Qing dynasty was finally toppled and a republic set up, although it was a republic mostly in name only. For some twenty years, China remained torn apart by factions, with warlords ruling some of the territories almost like independent kings. Gradually, two dominant groups emerged: the Kuomintang, later called the Nationalists, and the Communists.

Japan became a force in Manchuria and wanted to

exploit its rich natural resources. In 1932, the Japanese set up the puppet state of Manchukuo, with the deposed Manchu emperor, Pu Yi, as its head. In 1937, Japan began its invasion of the whole of China.

With the defeat of Japan in the Second World War, China regained its sovereignty. After the Communists took control of the country in 1949, the three provinces of Manchuria became an integral part of the People's Republic of China.

Although there are few pure Manchus left, some vestiges of the long Manchu rule can still be seen. Before the Manchu Qing dynasty, Chinese men and women wore robes open in front and held together with a wide sash, somewhat like a kimono. The slinky gown with slits, high collar, and buttons down one side is of Manchu origin. Called a *cheongsam* by the Cantonese and by foreigners, it is still called *qi pao*, "Manchu gown," by most mainland Chinese.

LENSEY NAMIOKA was born in Beijing and moved to the United States when she was a child. She is the author of many books for children, including *Ties That Bind, Ties That Break,* an ALA Best Book for Young Adults and the companion to *An Ocean Apart, a World Away.*

Her middle-grade novels include *Yang the Youngest and His Terrible Ear,* a Young Reader's Choice Award nominee; *Yang the Third and Her Impossible Family; Yang the Second and Her Secret Admirers; Yang the Eldest and His Odd Jobs;* and *April and the Dragon Lady,* a nominee for the Utah Young Adults' Book Award.

Lensey Namioka lives in Seattle with her family.